Winter *Swans*

DANICA WINTERS

author of *Montana Mustangs* and *The Nymph's Labyrinth*

CRIMSON ROMANCE

F+W Media, Inc.

This edition published by
Crimson Romance
an imprint of F+W Media, Inc.
10151 Carver Road, Suite 200
Blue Ash, Ohio 45242
www.crimsonromance.com

ISBN 10: 1-4405-6547-3
ISBN 13: 978-1-4405-6547-2
eISBN 10: 1-4405-6548-1
eISBN 13: 978-1-4405-6548-9

Cover art © 123rf.com

To Herbie—
Thank you for being so gracious, wonderful, kind, and loving.
I know it's not always easy to be married to a woman who has
her mind in an imaginary world.

Acknowledgments

To me there is nothing better than getting a letter from a fan telling me how much they've enjoyed my work. To all those wonderful fans out there who take the time from their busy lives to read and enjoy my books—Thank you. Your support and love is what keeps me writing on those days that the words are a struggle.

I hope that if you are in search of escape, or a break from the stresses of the real world, you can find what you need within the pages of my books.

I must also extend my thanks to my many author friends who take their time and energy to work with me in making my books the best they can possibly be. A special thank you to Casey Dawes, Rionna Morgan, Clare Woods, Pam Morris, John Zunski, Nancy and Parris Ja Young, Brooke Barnett, Kristi Fitzgerald, Heather Somerlad, Chris Karlsen, Jennifer Conner, Margret Best, and Melanie Calahan.

I would like to give a special thanks to my family, Herb, Penny, Bridget, and Gavin. Thank you for understanding that sometimes I have to sacrifice our time to follow the dream of writing.

Thank you to my lovely agent, Amanda Luedeke. You always work your tail off. Thank you for your constant support, back and forth emails, and phone calls. Above all, thank you for being a person I can trust.

And thanks couldn't be complete without thanking my editors: Jess Verdi, Julie Sturgeon, and Tara Gelsomino. Thank you for your hard work in bringing my projects to life.

Chapter One

The chapel of the funeral home was filled with familiar faces, each one drawn into a somber expression as they wandered past Harper Cygnini's sister's casket. A blonde nymph laid a single crystal swan inside the box, carefully placing the bird by the hundreds of others. The bird sat with its wings touching those of the one next to it, looking as if they would come alive and fly Jenna to the realm of the gods.

Harper stood at the head of the casket and shook hands as people passed by, never looking her in the eyes. There were no words to express the sadness that filled the room. This didn't happen. Nymphs rarely died.

She dabbed at her stinging eyes. She had cried so much in the last week it came as a shock to her there were any tears left to be shed. Her heart wasn't merely broken—no, the pain ran much deeper—it was almost as if she had died as well. Maybe she should have—the gods knew she deserved to be struck down. If she had just been more involved with her sister, if she had paid more attention, perhaps this would have never happened. She could have stopped her sister from being kidnapped. She would have noticed that Jenna had been missing. Instead Harper had merely gotten the call that Jenna's body had been found frozen in a snow bank on some mountain.

The only comfort she could find was that the men responsible had been incarcerated and awaited trial in Montana. They would pay for their atrocious crimes.

The only man in the room, Beau Morris, sat next to his fiancée, Ariadne Papadakis, the leader of the Sisterhood of Epione. Ariadne, noticing Harper's gaze, dipped her head in a humble tribute to Jenna. Harper recognized a few of the other women within the room as mustang, snake, and swan-shifters. It was easy to tell them from the non-supernatural attendees as, even in mourning, most nymphs were perfectly beautiful—unscathed by time and the ravages of living.

The same couldn't be said of Harper, but she didn't care. She glanced down at her black dress. She couldn't remember putting it on or doing her hair, but what did it matter? Even as a demigod life was short and filled with pain. What difference did her appearance really make—it was like so many other unimportant things that both humans and nymphs seemed to deem worthwhile. She couldn't strike the impious thought that life was only some god's sick joke—they merely sat up in the heavens playing around with everyone's lives, striking down those who displeased them and testing to see how much pain those that remained could withstand.

A hand touched her shoulder, making her jerk to attention.

"Harper?" a redheaded woman asked. She was beautiful and clearly a nymph, but she didn't have the same youthful, healthy glow of the others that filled the room. Instead her face was thin and her eyes tired.

"Yes. Thank you for coming to show your respect," she answered robotically as she readied herself for more well-deserved but undesired condolences.

"I'm Carey Jackson, a friend … I mean I *was* a friend of your sister."

The words pierced Harper's armor and drove straight to her heart. The tears stung her tired eyes. She could only nod, or any control she had would be lost.

Carey dropped her hand from Harper's shoulder. "I'm sorry to have to do this to you, but your sister was my landlord and, well, she promised she would help me. And now I don't have anyone to turn to, except you."

Harper looked around, checking to see if what she was hearing was really happening here, at her sister's funeral. Some of the pain she had been feeling dissipated and was replaced by red-hot anger. "You can't be serious. You didn't come here to ask for a favor. You didn't come to this place … and this time … and want to *use* my sister's death to your advantage. No one can be that callous."

The redhead stepped back from the onslaught of verbal strikes. "I'm … I'm sorry. I didn't mean to upset you. I just need help. You don't understand."

Harper's gaze dropped to Jenna. Her makeup was perfectly applied and her pale face unmoving, as if she had merely fallen asleep. Her brunette hair haloed around her and, even though she lay there in the white metal box, it was still hard to believe she was really gone.

Carey reached into her purse and pulled out a picture. "I'm looking for this man. I need to find him, it's important. Please."

Harper didn't know what to say. She knew her anger toward the woman was based mostly in her own grief. The redhead needed help, even if she had made a mistake in approaching her here on this day.

Carey offered her the picture. Harper looked down at the image—the man was muscular and tan, almost the color of fresh honey. His copper-tinted brown hair framed his face and accentuated his stubble-covered jaw. He was laughing at some secret joke that had been lost in time and only his smile was preserved. She flipped over the picture and scrawled across the back was the name Chance Landon.

"Look," she started. "I don't think I can help … " She glanced up, but the redhead was gone. The next mourner in line, a petite woman with a sharp beak-like nose, stepped forward.

"Where … " Harper looked past the mousy haired woman in front of her in search of the mysterious redhead.

"Excuse me?" the mousy woman said with an out-of-place smile.

"Yes, sorry," Harper said, forcing herself to look at the gray business suit clad woman in front of her. The top button of the woman's white dress shirt was fastened and there wasn't a wrinkle to be seen anywhere on her perfectly put together outfit. "Thank you for coming." The practiced words tumbled from her lips.

"You are welcome. I just wanted to introduce myself. I'm Dr. Redbird. I was the chief medical examiner on your sister's case."

Harper tried to keep the shock from striking her down. So many emotions invaded her all at once. Anger. Pain. Resentment. Thankfulness. "What are you doing here?"

The woman's smile flickered and she glanced over her shoulder, like she was looking for some kind of attack. "I just wanted to say how sorry I am for your sister's death. I thought I would pay my last respects to her family … and your kind."

Something about the woman seemed *off*, but then again everything that was happening in Harper's life didn't seem to fit. She'd never prepared herself to be standing in a room full of acquaintances, mourners, and a favor-asking redhead—especially when they were all there to pay respects to her sister, a woman she had thought would never die.

Chapter Two

The lawyer waited in his office at the far end of the desolate hall. A dark romance style painting of a couple in an olive-colored meadow hung crooked on the wall. As Harper passed the lopsided image she was struck by the way that not only the couple, but even the picture, seemed to grieve.

Harper ran her finger over her pocket where Chance Landon's picture was hidden. Why had the strange redhead, Carey, been looking for the man? Had he done something wrong? Had the woman done something wrong? She had been so desperate, but did Harper really want to get involved?

The door to the office stood ajar and inside sat a black-suited lawyer with a dour face and a paunch belly. She pushed open the door further and the lawyer looked up. "Ms. Cygnini, it's so nice to see you again. I'm only sorry it has to be under these particular circumstances."

She always hated seeing the man with the pinched face, the last time she had seen Mr. Singer was when she had signed her divorce papers. She owed him for keeping all of her and Jenna's secrets, and he knew it—which made this meeting all the worse. "Thanks for meeting with me on such short notice. I know you'd rather have met next week, but I appreciate you understanding I want to get this over with."

"I completely understand." He reached down and pulled a file from his briefcase. "I'll make this as painless as possible."

She tried to stop from wincing at Mr. Singer's poorly chosen words. The lawyer must have known she was in a great deal of pain—each pitying look, each "I'm sorry" carved a slice from her ever shrinking heart. Soon there would be nothing left for the masses to take … and nothing left for her to give.

She tried to stuff away her misgivings toward the man. He was only doing his job. "That would be preferable."

He sat the file down on his desk, next to a single crystal swan, which collected the dust-filled light given off by a small desk lamp. "I must apologize for not making it to the services for Jenna. I had other obligations." He slid the swan across the table. "Accept this with my apologies."

Harper took the swan with a nod and carefully placed the glass bird in her purse and out of the presence of the undeserving man.

"When do you have to return to work at Merckson?"

"They want me back to Seattle next week. They're working on a new drug and need me there when the clinical testing is finalized."

He flipped open the file. "That isn't much time."

She couldn't disagree more. The snow-covered hills of Worley, Idaho were starting to wear on her. She missed the beautiful green mountains and the sound of rain on the roof of her house. "I think it will be more than enough time to settle my sister's affairs. She couldn't have had that much."

"Your sister had become a bit of a lost soul, hadn't she?"

Another slice fell away from her heart. "Recently she had been making some questionable choices."

Harper couldn't help but think of Jenna's last poor choice in trying to get pregnant, something a nymph hadn't been able to do in the last hundred years.

"If it makes you feel any better, she was cash poor but asset rich at the time of her death. And as her will states, she left most of her assets to you. You could have a secure future."

Harper didn't care about her sister's money, even if the lawyer did. Money was nothing more than another thing to accrue— she'd been alive long enough to have her fair share. She would give it all away if it meant getting her sister back. Money didn't matter. Only blood. Family. Sisterhood. Now all she had was her extended family of nymphs. She was affable with a few, but now Jenna was gone she felt alone.

The soulless lawyer flipped another page. "There was some real estate left to you. There is a home near Worley and an apartment complex by Coeur d'Alene." He pulled out a few papers and slid them across the table. "Here are the rental agreements and the list of tenants. She was running the building on her own, but I recommend you find a property management company if you need to return to your job in Seattle."

"Thanks, I'll look into it." Harper took the papers and scanned over the list of names. Halfway down the list she found the name she was looking for. Carey Jackson, apartment 316. The mysterious woman at the funeral had been telling her the truth. She had been Jenna's tenant.

"Jenna left one thing to an outside party." The lawyer tapped his finger on the paper, interrupting her thoughts. He stared down at the paper, and read out loud. "I, Jenna Cygnini, leave my collection of antique leather-bound books to one Ms. Carey Jackson, or her descendant, contingent upon the recipient being of a sufficient age (eighteen or older), to have proper reverence for, and responsibly put to use said texts."

"What does that mean, exactly?" Harper reached over and motioned for the paper.

"You'll need to find the books and get them to Carey Jackson." Extending the page, the lawyer handed it over. The words were exactly as he'd read them. Her breath rushed from her. Why was everything, even her sister's will, pointing to this woman?

"What happens if I don't find these books?"

"Then the matter will remain open and, upon their being found, they must be turned over to the named party," the lawyer said offhandedly. He drew open his desk drawer and pulled out a manila envelope. Keys jingled inside the paper as he slid it across the desk. "Inside you will find another copy of the will, the deeds to your sister's properties, the keys to her home, and her autopsy report. I just need you to sign some papers and this matter will be handled."

Yes, the assets Jenna had left her would be under her care, but this *matter* was far from being *handled*. The agony of her sister's death would fill her heart for eternity.

•••

The key slid into the lock as if it knew it was home, but Harper didn't feel the same excitement. Sucking in a long breath, she twisted the key and the bolt slid open with a hollow metallic click that reminded her of the sound of Jenna's coffin being shut. The thought drew chills down her spine.

Her hands shook as she turned the handle and pushed the door open to her sister's house. The stale air of a house closed up too long rushed out, as if it begged to be released from its sorrowful isolation.

Searching on the wall, she found a switch and flicked on the lights. Dust covered the side table next to the door. Amidst the dust sat a stack of unopened mail and a key ring filled with dozens of keys, small and large, zebra striped and covered in plastic, simple brass and aluminum. The funny array of mismatched and haphazardly arranged keys brought a smile to her lips. They reminded her so much of her sister in the way they seemed to be in a beautiful pattern of disarray.

It struck her that these mismatched keys, in their disheveled state, were perhaps some of the last things Jenna had touched.

She sat the packet of papers the lawyer had given her on the table next to the key ring as if the simple action would somehow bring her closer to Jenna. She was careful to leave her sister's touch undisturbed.

Harper's footsteps echoed through the house as she made her way to the living room. The lonely sound made the heaviness in her heart grow. She couldn't stand the quiet—it was too much, almost as if it was the universe's way of reminding her she would be alone for the rest of time. Picking up the dust-covered remote, she clicked on the television to a local channel and let the noise cover the painful silence.

There was nothing in this place she wanted to keep or take home to Seattle, at least nothing she could see in the living room. She simply needed to find the collection of antique books and get the house and apartment on the market, and all the loose ends would be handled. Then Harper could head back to Seattle and find some respite in her routine.

On the bookshelf in the corner of the living room, Harper found a vast array of worn romance novels. She pulled one out. The cover was a 1970s drawing of a woman with a Farrah Fawcett hairstyle of backward rolls and frosted strands. She remembered the book from the days she and her sister had spent together, talking and laughing about the events of their lives—it wasn't too many years later they had moved apart and found their own life paths. Even though she knew she was being silly, she couldn't stop herself from pulling the well-read book to her chest and embracing it for the memories it held.

She slumped onto the couch and flipped through the yellowed pages. On the title page was Jenna's looping and messy handwriting that read: *From Harper, 1979.*

Before she realized it, Harper had started to read the book, but the noise of the television drew her attention. There was a commercial for a poker game at the local bar and casino. As she watched the lights shift, she caught a glimpse of a familiar face. There, sitting at a poker table, was Chance Landon. Her heart lurched.

He was even more handsome than the man in the picture. From the fine lines on his face, it was clear he had grown older since the picture had been taken, but there was no denying he was the same person Carey had been looking for. The book dropped into Harper's lap and she stared at the screen until the advertisement was replaced and the man had once again disappeared.

Her lungs ached before she remembered to breathe. She couldn't help but think the commercial was another sign that she was meant to find the handsome stranger.

Using the DVR, she skipped backward and watched the ad again. She made a mental note of the address for the poker game, which would take place in an hour at the Cellar Casino. It seemed easy enough to pop down to the bar and give the man the message that Carey had been looking for him. He could make of it what he may, but at least Harper wouldn't have the crazy woman and her desperate plea on her mind any longer. She could wash her hands of the entire situation. And besides, it would give her a reason to get out of this house, and away from the haunting memories that filled the place.

She made a quick dash out to her car, grabbed her suitcase, and brought it upstairs to the largest guest bedroom. The door to her sister's bedroom was closed. And as badly as she wanted to be done with it all and away from here, she couldn't bring herself to open the door. She wasn't ready to go through her things, to smell her sister's familiar scent of citrus and cloves. Maybe while she was at the bar she would get a drink to dull the pain of sorting through Jenna's precious things.

On the wall, next to the guest bathroom, was a picture of Harper and Jenna in the 1920s. They were smiling with painted pink cheeks and beaded dresses. Each of them wore a feather in her hair and stood proudly exposing bare legs, which had only made the Victorian era people judge them as rebels and feminist thrill-seekers. Jenna had loved every minute of throwing away the repressive trappings of the previous era. Their finest moment had come with the active bootlegging of socially required, but unaccepted, whiskey. So much had changed since then. In a way, Harper felt old. She'd given up so much—her spontaneity, her zest for life, her freedom—all since she and Jenna had put another person between them over twenty years ago.

In the bathroom, Harper readied herself for a shower. Moving to the tub, she turned on the water and let it run over her tired hands. Her mind drifted around the events of the day until the heat of the water seeped into her flesh, reviving her sorrow-numbed skin. She pulled the metal tap that turned on the shower and she was met with a strangled sound of metal banging within the wall. The pipe's complaint grew louder and no water escaped the aged showerhead. Fearing the shower would break, she turned off the tap.

Even the house was pushing for her to be on her way. Harper turned to the mirror and caught a glimpse of her tired eyes. On the shelf just beneath the mirror was a man's razor and shaving cream.

Harper picked up the razor—from the look of the edge it had been well used. Who had Jenna been seeing? The only man at the memorial had been Beau Morris. Did the man who used this razor not know Jenna was dead? Or did he know and simply not care? There was so much she hadn't known about Jenna's new life.

Another sliver of Harper's heart slipped away.

Chapter Three

The casino was illuminated by glaring red lights and the flash of slot machines. Harper weaved her way through the maze of machines and attendants with fluorescent-glazed smiles. A crowd of players and bystanders swarmed around two well-lit poker tables that ran adjacent to the back wall.

Moving between two onlookers at the center of the activity, she spotted the copper brown-haired man who matched the picture in her pocket. She had practiced what she was going to say to the man, but now that she was here and so close, she couldn't remember what she had planned on saying.

The carpet seemed to reach up and clench her feet, making it hard for her to move. Chance was laughing again, looking much like he had in the picture—and once again she was oblivious to the joke.

Forcing her body to move, she stepped toward him. He looked up and for the first time she could see his strong, steely eyes. He was talking, but his ever-so-kissable pink lips turned up into a devilish grin. The deafening tweets and rings of the machines were muted by the thundering of her heart. Without thinking, her lips pulled into a coy smile, returning his affections.

She took another step and her foot connected with something, sending her into a free fall. Her face hit a barstool and she tumbled sideways until she landed on the floor. The pain in her chin, coupled with her embarrassment, brought tears to her eyes.

She mentally kicked herself. He was just a man, albeit a good-looking one, and she was a nymph—she should have been far above the fumbling of a love-struck teenager.

Her gaze was pinned to the floor as gasps, whispered insults, and mocking laughs echoed through the voiceless room.

Harper's cheeks flamed and a thin veil of sweat rose to her skin. There was no playing off what she had done. She closed her eyes and willed her body to disappear, but she went nowhere.

Black cowboy boots appeared in front of her. "Excuse me, ma'am. Are you okay?" The man's voice was a smooth lulling drawl of a man who, even in crisis, kept an even temper.

Not only was she hurt and lying on a dirty floor surrounded by professional gamblers, people who made it an art to hide their faults, but she also had the added humiliation of lying at the feet of a cowboy. Her body tingled with the urge to shift, to turn into her swan form and fly away from the scene she had caused. Yet now wasn't the time to be a coward—she'd screwed up and had to face the firing squad of snickering bystanders.

The boots shuffled and a hand appeared in front of her face. "Let me help you up."

Harper couldn't avoid it any longer; she slipped her hand into the rough callused fingers. Stars filled her vision as he pulled her to standing—though she couldn't be sure if it was the sudden motion or the strange charge of the touch that whispered through her body and spoke to her soul. It was Chance.

As the stars cleared, all she could see were his mesmerizing eyes. They were light gray with a dark gray ring—as if his eyes were made with the strength of steel and imbued with the power of the gods.

An onlooker cleared his throat, breaking the moment. She'd only hated Jenna's killer more.

The man dropped her hand and turned to the crowd. "There's nothing to see here. The lady's fine. Go back to what you were doing."

The crowd of people went back to their conversations, and Harper couldn't help but notice the way some of the women kept glancing furtively over in Chance's direction.

"You okay?"

"I'm fine, though I feel like an idiot."

"You took one heck of a fall. You sure you're okay?"

The warmth in her cheeks returned. "I swear. Just embarrassed."

"Well there are only a few people that could have won a fight with a barstool." The sound of Chance's deep laugh brought a strange lurching motion to her core and drove deeper, to more explicit places.

"What can I say? I guess I'm not gifted at barstool handling."

He gave her a grin. "That's no great shame, just so long as you are good at handling other things." His cheeks went ruddy and a thin sheen of sweat broke on his forehead. "I'm sorry … I didn't mean it … not like that … I only meant … " he stammered.

Even being inadvertently lewd, he was irresistibly cute and she couldn't help the giggle that tumbled from her lips like an invitation for him to keep flirting.

Their little interlude couldn't continue. Harper had to put a stop to the flirtation—she had no time or place in her life for a man and all the drama a relationship would encompass.

"I didn't mean to interrupt your game. I just saw you on television and … "

"You saw us on TV? That's great. They told me they'd put it up in time to draw more players." He turned to a pudgy, balding man by the table. "Hey, Kodie, this lady here said she saw us on television. Good job, man!"

The man expanded like an excited puffer fish and made his way to the cowboy's side. "See? I can pull a few strings." The man jabbed his chubby thumbs in the small pockets of his buttoned vest. "It's nice to meet you. I'm Kodie and this famous guy here is my friend Chance Landon—the best poker player in the United States."

"Kodie, please knock it off," Chance said, embarrassed over the man's gushing.

"It's true, ain't it? Ain't nothing to be ashamed of as far as I'm concerned. I'm damn proud." Kodie's smile grew impossibly wider. "What's your name? Did you come down to get his autograph? I have a feeling they're going to be selling for quite a few bucks before long."

Did the man ever stop talking?

"I'm Harper. I just wanted to stop by and talk to Chance really quick. If you don't mind, I'm going to just steal him away for a sec and then you can have him right back."

"Well, don't steal him for too long, he has a game starting soon. He needs to keep up his strength." Kodie gave her a suggestive wink.

"Oh hell, he just can't stop, can he?" Chance took her gently by the arm and led her to a far corner where a few poker machines sat empty. "I'm sorry about him. He's just excited about the game— we got on a good turn of the cards tonight."

"Is he your manager?"

Chance laughed. "No, we just run together. Sometimes he helps wrangle up games for us when we come to town."

She gave him a sideways glance. "Are you two hustlers or card sharks or something?"

"Nah, we're just here to play a few hands and then we'll be on our way again." He gave her a pitying smile. "We're leaving for Las Vegas in the next day or two."

The air filled with the tinny sound of the slots and an awkward silence.

"You said you came here to tell me something?"

"I … " She drifted off, troubled by the news that he'd be leaving soon.

"It's alright if you don't remember. You're welcome to stick around until you do, but I need to get back to the tables." He turned on the heel of his boot as he moved to walk away.

The action drew her out of her stupor. "Sorry … I just … It must have been the fall. I'm not feeling well," she lied. "I just came to tell you that I ran into a woman who was looking for you."

"What woman?"

"She said her name was Carey Jackson."

"Who?" he asked, as if he hadn't heard the name.

"Carey, Carey Jackson."

"That's what I thought you said." His shoulders dropped. "Look, I don't know what lies my ex-wife was telling, but I'm sorry she bothered you. She's a whole heap of trouble that no one needs in their life—especially someone like you, the woman who trips over chairs." There was a forced playful edge to his voice.

Jealousy crept up her back like bony fingers. Carey had been his wife?

"She seemed pretty upset over something. But you can make of it what you will." Harper reached in her back pocket and took out a slip of paper with the phone number she had retrieved from the rental agreement, and the picture Carey had given her. "Here's her number. She doesn't live far from here. Plus, I think you should have this back," she said, motioning to his picture.

Chance took the picture and paper, grazing her hand. He stuffed the papers into his shirt pocket. "Thanks. And hey, since I'm going to be in town for a few more days, maybe we could meet up? You could tell me a little bit more about what Carey told you."

"If you want to see me again, my phone number is on the slip."

Harper's body shivered as his wanting eyes caressed her body. There was only so much a sex-starved nymph could handle before she crumbled.

Chapter Four

The piece of paper Harper had given him was just that—a simple piece of paper. Nothing more. Yet Chance couldn't understand what all it meant. It didn't seem likely that she was picking him up, no … not a woman like her. Harper must have been trying to help Carey, but why? Why had Harper agreed to help his ex-wife in finding him? And why was Carey looking for him? It had been over seventeen years since he'd heard from her. Sure, he still thought of Carey and would have liked to have gone back in time and ended things differently, but there was no point in regret. They were done. Or so he had thought.

A pile of wrinkled clothes lay on the bed next to his rucksack and he rifled through them until his little black cell phone fell from the pocket of the shirt he had worn the day before. There was just enough battery life left to make a call or two—even if it was a call he didn't want to make. He pressed the numbers, and the phone rang until it mercifully went to her voicemail.

"Hey, Carey. Just got a message you were looking for me. This's my new number. Give me a call so I don't worry." He hung up the phone, but couldn't help feeling like a bit of a dumbass—why did he say he would worry?

He dumped his phone into his bag and it landed on top of his checkbook. Carey was going to read a whole lot more into the message than what he wanted. Maybe he shouldn't have called her. No. It would have bothered him. He had to call, but why did he have to say something so idiotic?

Dammit. He didn't even want to open the door of possibility of them getting back together.

His mind wandered to the time they'd spent together. They'd both been in their early twenties when they'd married. For a while, things had been good. He thought she'd understood his lifestyle and how important the game was to him. He'd explained his past. How in every relationship he'd had, the women had wanted him to change—they loved the romance of a famous drifter, but when the novelty wore off they all wanted a man who was stable—a man who wanted to settle down, raise a family, the whole white-picket-fence thing.

He'd thought, with Carey being a nymph, that she could understand his traveling and inability to settle down. For a year, she had traveled with him, enjoying the perks of his lifestyle and fame. But that time had been enough for her to decide that the life he lived was too much, and she'd given him an ultimatum—give up poker, or she was gone.

It hadn't been an easy decision.

As Harper's handwriting stared up at him from the slip of paper still in his hand, Chance couldn't help but wonder if she was a nymph like Carey. She was certainly beautiful enough to be one, but asking her if she was a supernatural being was out of the question. She'd think he was crazy if she wasn't one, and if she was a nymph it was her secret to share—or not.

Nymph or not, he wondered if Harper was the kind of woman who would want him to change or if she was the kind who went with the flow—who took one day at a time. He flipped the paper over in his fingers. Her letters were tight and even, not the writing of a woman who was relaxed or spontaneous, but he could have had her all wrong.

Maybe he should call Harper and see if there was anything else she knew that could help him decipher Carey's cloak-and-dagger request to find him. If nothing else, it would give him the chance to talk to Harper again. She had been so damn cute, even lying there on the red-checkered carpet of the casino floor.

He smiled as he recalled the way she had looked up at him, like she was a little fragile bird desperately in need of saving—and in a way she had been. The people who had surrounded her were ruthless, and the most successful of them seemed to be devoid of normal human emotion. It was what made them good at the game. He wished he could've been as unemotional as they were—but something about seeing the fallen bird had pulled at his heartstrings. There'd been no other choice but come to her aid.

There was a quick rap of knuckles against the hotel door followed by a click and beep of a keycard. The door opened and Kodie walked in. "What're you doing? You ready to go?"

"If you mean go to get some coffee, yes."

"Well, we can start with coffee, but don't you think we should be hitting the road? Vegas awaits."

Chance ran his fingers over the black-inked letters on the paper. "Why don't we stay another night? It would give you a chance to win some money."

"I thought you said you wanted to get out of this hell-hole." Kodie leaned up against the cheap particleboard desk, which served as the shabby room's catchall. "Or does our staying have something to do with that little brunette number I saw you talking to, little Miss Trips-A-Lot?"

Chance chuckled. "She told me Carey's looking for me."

"Damn. Sorry to hear it." His friend grimaced. "Are you sure you don't want to leave today?"

"Nah, I gotta see what she needs. Besides, after watching how you played last night, it looks like you are going to need another night to win your money back. "

Kodie's face puckered in response to the ribbing. "You just had a lucky turn of the cards and you and I both know why."

"And you know that luck can only take you so far."

"That's true, man, but my table wasn't running as hot. I could have used some of your luck last night." The desk under Kodie squeaked as he shifted uncomfortably. "But no worries. I'll get the money to pay that nut-buster, Nate, back. You know how it is."

Actually, Chance didn't. He never borrowed money and he had never been mixed up with the dirty dealings of Three-Eyed Nate—at least not until he'd been pulled into Kodie's bullshit after his friend had lost everything at the World Poker Tournament and had turned to Nate for the two hundred thousand dollars he'd needed to buy back in.

"Kodie, why don't I just give you the money to pay back Three-Eyed Nate? If I give you the money I was going to use for the tournament buy-in, you would have enough to pay him back."

"There's three million dollars or more at stake. I can't have you walking away from that kind of money, especially not when I know you're gonna win the tournament. And besides, I'm not borrowing any more money." Kodie stepped closer. "I'll just pick up a few games in Vegas while you are playing in the tournament. Hopefully I can pull enough money together to pay Nate back."

Kodie was living on a dream. There was no way he could make enough money while they were in Vegas … the man had been on a losing streak. Kodie couldn't play the game with a straight face when there was a large sum of money at stake. He'd always been too easy to get riled up—it was one of the reasons he'd lost at the World Poker Tournament, and why he'd have to act only as Chance's corner man at the upcoming Champions of Poker Tournament in Vegas. There were too many emotions for Kodie to stay calm and in the game. There were too many blank stares and silent prayers for the river to flip and rain down the card the player so desperately wanted to see.

"How about this?" Chance paused as he thought for a second. "You let me stay one more night and then if I win in Vegas, we split the pot? You can consider it a commission for being my assistant."

"Assistant, my ass," Kodie said, his voice carrying an edge of relief. "I'm the one who taught you how to play the game."

Chance's laughter filled the room. "So you'll take the deal?"

The desk thumped against the wall as Kodie pushed to standing. "If we're gonna stay here another night, I'm gonna need to get ready for tonight's game—man's gotta get his beauty sleep in order to play well. You know what I always say, *if your mind's a mess so is your game.*"

"I think you're well past the point of benefiting from a little beauty sleep."

"Ha, ha, ha—real funny, jackass. You wanna meet up before the game, talk about a little strategy?"

Chance flicked the paper against his other hand. "Nah, I think I'll have to catch you later. I need to make some phone calls. But hey … if it's strategy you're looking for, here it is—don't lose." He gave Kodie a wide grin, fully aware he was pushing his friend's buttons.

"You better hope you're not going to be playing against me tonight. I'll take you down."

"I'm sure you would, but I don't know if I'm going to get into tonight's game," Chance hesitated as he searched for a credible excuse. "I don't want to use up all my luck—not with the tournament coming up. Want to save up a little bit of it for the big day."

"That's good. You can kick Three-Eyed Nate's ass and split the pot with me. I'll pay him back and it'll be handled." Kodie walked to the door and clicked open the lock.

"You know time's running out. He's going to be gunning for you." Chance hated to think of what Three-Eyed Nate would do to Kodie if his friend didn't get the money he needed to pay back the loan shark. "What happens if I lose, Kodie? What are you going to do?"

"Come on now, man. You're the best poker player in the world. You got it in the bag," Kodie said, but there was a flicker of concern in his eyes as he turned and pulled the door open.

Chance cringed.

"And don't worry, once I pay him back, I won't be taking calling in any more favors. Not if I can help it."

"I'd rather you ask for favors instead of Carey."

"I guess even you can't have all the luck." Kodie smirked. "Have fun dealing with her bullshit. If you need me, I'll be here."

"Thanks, man."

The door closed behind Kodie as Chance retrieved his phone out of his rucksack. Before he left for Vegas, he needed to know more about the situation with Carey—and see if she was merely up to her old bag of tricks. He dropped down on to the bed and stared at the numbers to reach Harper. After a moment, he punched the numbers on the paper into his phone. The phone rang.

"Hello?" Harper answered.

He cleared his throat, unsure of exactly what he should say. "Hi. How's it going? Your chin okay?"

There was a long silence. "Who is this?" she finally answered.

"Sorry," he said with an awkward laugh. "This is Chance. Chance Landon? We met yesterday. At the casino."

The pause from the other end of the line made a thin film of sweat rise in his hand.

"Yes, Chance. I know who you are," she said, her voice growing higher in pitch. "I'm surprised you called."

He was shocked. Didn't most men she gave her number to call? Or did she not give out her number very often? He hoped for the latter.

"Well, I wanted to talk to you a little more about Carey. I tried to get a hold of her this evening, but she didn't answer her phone."

Harper sucked in a breath. "I'm working on some things right now, why don't you meet me at my sister's house?"

He grabbed a pen and wrote down the address she gave him on the hotel's stationary.

"And hey," she continued. "You aren't some serial killer or something, are you? I can trust you, right?"

He snickered. "If I were a serial killer I think it would be a little too late to ask the question—I already have your address."

"Wow, that's a lot of confidence you just instilled in me."

"If it makes you feel better, I'm not that kind of man. You have nothing to worry about from me." He caught himself. "I mean as long as you don't gamble."

"Nope. Not a gambler."

It was too bad. He would have liked for her to take a gamble on him.

Chapter Five

Specks of dust splashed up into the thin sunbeam streaming through the curtains of the long neglected spare bedroom. The specks danced in lonely circles as Harper sat the collapsed cardboard moving boxes she carried onto the floor.

The roar of a truck echoed through the still room as it pulled into the driveway. She stood up and peered out of the window, careful to stay behind the drapes so Chance couldn't see her watching. Hopefully he wasn't anticipating getting any wealth of knowledge from her about Carey. For all she knew the woman could have been a princess or a fraud—the man had to know more about her than she did.

He looked strikingly handsome in his western style denim jacket, and the fur collar accented his well-loved white cowboy hat. The hat was so low she couldn't see his eyes or the medium length brown locks that lay underneath.

Chance stopped on the path that led up to the front door and rearranged his jacket as if he was shaking away his nerves. The simple action brought a smile to Harper's face. Maybe he hadn't come here only with the intention of learning more about Carey. Maybe it was possible he had come here to learn about Harper as well. It was a silly, immature hope that he would be interested in her, and Harper tried to tamper the thought as she made her way downstairs.

When she was halfway down the creaking steps, there was a knock at the door, but she didn't speed up.

She stopped behind the door and took in a long breath. He'd only come with questions, nothing more.

There was another rap of his knuckles against the door. "Harper? You home?"

She slid back the lock and opened the front door. "Hi, Chance. Sorry to keep you waiting, I was just upstairs trying to get started on boxing up the house."

"No problem. You need help?"

"No, but thanks. This's my sister's house. I'm just getting things in order to sell. Why don't you come in?"

There was a moment of awkward silence as he walked in and stood by the door. "Um, thanks."

Some of her nerves melted away. If he was here to sweep her off her feet, he was making a poor showing. She had been silly to read her own daft hopes into the meaning of his visit.

"So what would you like to know?" She was so uncomfortable around him, her toes curled. "I mean about Carey. I promise I told you everything she told me."

"I'm sure." He glanced around the room like he was lost in the small 1950s two-story house. "Where's your sister? Is she coming back tonight to help you get things ready for the sale?"

The pain of his words was immediate. People had to keep pulling at the stitches she had put on her heart and reopening the painful wound of her sister's untimely demise. Maybe she needed to wear a sign that read *Yes, my sister is dead.* Maybe people would leave her alone and she could sequester the pain away.

"My sister, Jenna, died a few weeks ago in Montana. I just came down for the services and to get all of her affairs in order before I get back to work."

His tight, nervous expression went slack. "Oh my God, Harper. I'm so sorry. I didn't know."

"It's okay," she lied. "It's all going to be taken care of soon. Then I can get back to Seattle."

"Seattle, huh?"

"The Emerald City."

"I thought that was in *The Wizard of Oz.*"

She couldn't control the laugh that slipped from her tired body. "Yes, like Oz. There's no place like home." She clicked her heels.

He gave a quick nervous laugh as he pulled off his cowboy hat, revealing his disheveled locks. He dropped his arm and curled the brim in his fingertips. Watching him stand there at full nervous attention, she couldn't help the feeling that she was making him endure some kind of mental torture—even a human man had to feel the emotional weight of this mournful place.

"Hey, why don't we get out of here?" She offered. "I need a break. I've been working all day."

His fingers relaxed on the brim of his hat. "That would be great. What are you hungry for?"

She was hungry for a lot of things; she was hungry for escape, hungry for a task that would take her mind off Jenna's death, and more than anything she was hungry to get back home and back to work—but he didn't need to know anything about how much she hurt. "Is there a nice French restaurant close? I could really use a baguette and maybe a little basil salmon terrine." Her mouth watered as she thought of her favorite dish. "In Seattle I get it every Tuesday."

He reached into his back pocket and pulled out his phone. "Hold on, let me just call the butler and the chauffeur." Laughing at his ill-witted joke, he stuffed the phone back into his pocket and glanced up at her for validation of his humor.

It wasn't hard to hold back her smile.

"Come on now, I was just kidding. Can't you take a week off?" he asked with a slight tone of remorse. "I don't think we have many choices. I only saw a fast food joint and a buffet place a few miles back. I don't think they have anything that fancy around here—they're not quite up to Seattle standards."

She tried to control the anger as it clambered up from the depths of her soul. If he didn't like her for who and what she was, than he had no business spending any more time with her. "Look.

I may be a little stuck in my ways, but I find comfort in things I can control. If you can't appreciate that, then why don't you just ask me what you came here for and be on your way?"

He stepped back at the attack. "I was only kidding. Don't be upset with me. I didn't mean to be rude."

Guilt filled her. He had only been playing. He hadn't meant anything—she'd been too harsh. "You're right. I'm sorry, Chance."

She ran her hands over her face and down her hair. "I know you didn't mean anything. I'm just exhausted."

He dropped his hat on the table by the door, next to Jenna's keys. "Here, why don't you sit down and take a break. Maybe we can go out later?"

Chance grabbed her hand, and his fingers curled around hers as if he had touched her a thousand times before. He led her to the couch and made her sit down. She thought to resist, but her tired body didn't want to fight his kindness. Moving to the recliner, he grabbed a crocheted blanket and laid it across her lap. "Here. Just take a break. I'll make us some dinner and we can talk."

She gave him a weak smile. "I'm afraid there isn't much in the house."

"I'm a bachelor." Chance smiled brightly. "If there's a bottle of ketchup and some cheese I can make something for us to eat."

He wasn't here to antagonize her, only to be a friend—in fact, her only friend.

"Thanks, Chance."

He dipped his head like he was dipping his cowboy hat in acknowledgment. "We all have tough days. And losing a loved one is about the toughest days of them all."

Chance turned and walked into the kitchen. The sounds of cupboards opening and shutting and a few muttered obscenities filtered out into the living room.

A little flutter rose up from her belly and her body clenched—the sensation came as a shock. It had been a long time since she had felt anything like this—this desire. She brushed the feelings off. It was only her nymphish desires playing tricks on her.

"Harper?" he called out, but his voice was off, drawing her concern.

"What?"

"I think you should come in here."

Throwing off the blanket, she got up and strode toward the kitchen. "Is she out of ketchup? I'm telling you maybe it's better if we go out." Turning the corner, Chance came into view. In his hand was a box of popcorn shrimp. "Oh, it's not salmon terrine, but at least shrimp are in the same realm," she said, passing him a weak smile. "I think she keeps her … I mean I think she *kept* her cookie sheets down—"

"We won't need a cookie sheet." Chance tipped the opened box and a white bag slid out and into his hand. "Do you know what this is?"

The bag was taped shut. "I'm guessing it isn't shrimp?"

Chance held out his hand so she could more closely inspect the square. "Far from it. From what I know about drugs, which ain't much, I think it's heroin."

Harper sucked in a breath. She knew Jenna had gotten involved with some less than seemly characters of late, but she hadn't known exactly how far her sister had fallen.

Chance pushed the square back into the blue box. "Did you know?"

"That my sister had a real taste for popcorn shrimp?" She tried in vain to make light of the situation, but from the look on Chance's face there was no easy way out. "No," she answered. "I didn't know. We had a bit of a falling out a few years ago and I hadn't seen her since. I've just been hearing things about her, and up to this point I was hoping that most of them had been distorted by hearsay. I guess people weren't too far off."

"Unfortunately I don't think they were."

She took the box and lifted out the square. "And you're wrong, this isn't heroin. I don't know what it is, but heroin is normally brown or black if it's high quality."

"Oh, really? Do you know about drugs?"

"It happens to be my job. I'm a pharmacologist. I work with drugs for a living. I know how to make them, test them, and sell them to the public. The only thing I don't do is use them."

"Well if you know so much, how do you think we should go about getting rid of this stuff?"

The box was heavy in her hands. There were a few ways they could get rid of the drugs, but Harper wasn't sure getting rid of it was the right move. Not until she understood everything. Not until she could understand what her sister had been doing with them.

Jenna couldn't have needed the drugs, not as a nymph—most drugs had little effect. She had to have been selling. And if she was selling, she had to have a dealer. Harper thought of the razor and shaving supplies upstairs on the bathroom counter. The way the razor had been laid out on the sink was as if whoever had used it had thought he was coming back. If the dealer had known Jenna had been killed, he would have come already and gotten all signs of himself and his drugs out of her house—or at the very least he would have tried to get all of his drugs out so he could sell them to someone else.

Her mind was going crazy and moving into the realm of asinine. Jenna wouldn't have dated a drug dealer. At least not the Jenna she had known.

"So?" Chance asked, pulling her from the melee of her thoughts.

"Sorry, I was just thinking."

"You weren't thinking about snorting it, were you?" He passed her a wicked grin.

"Like I said, I don't use drugs. I let others do that." She forced a tired smile. "I think we should call the police and let them know that we have found a stash."

"I don't think getting the police involved is the right idea. I mean, your sister's already passed, what good would come of dragging her memory into a drug raid?"

He was right, but she couldn't come to terms with not letting someone know that they had found a stash of unknown drugs. "I'm sure they wouldn't do a full investigation."

"Really?" He leaned back against the counter, resting his hands on the mustard-yellow laminate. "You haven't had much experience with law enforcement, have you?"

"To be honest, the only time I've talked to the police was when they notified me about my sister's death."

Chance reached out and waited for her to hand him the box. "Let me tell you something about the police. I mean, I have the utmost respect for most of them, but they are only about the job. Everything has to be done in redundancy—and here, in this small Idaho town, where there isn't much on the social spectrum for scandal—something like this will most certainly make the news. Everyone will want to know about your sister and her past." He pushed the tabs on the box shut. "And from what you've told me about Jenna, I don't think you'd want her truth to be known."

She let out a long sigh. He was correct, but not just in the sense that she didn't want her sister's activities to be broadcast—she couldn't let the media get close enough to notice the peculiarities that came with a nymph's past.

"If you let me, I have an idea." Chance tucked the box under his arm and then took her hand. "Why don't we go into the bathroom and dump it down the toilet? That way no one can get their hands on the drugs and no one can trace them back to this house or your sister, or worse—you."

Chapter Six

The water in the toilet bowl swirled, carrying what was probably thousands of dollars' worth of drugs down the drain. Harper dumped the empty box into the bin next to the commode.

"Well, we have that taken care of," she said, wiping her hands together, "but I'm still hungry. Why don't we just go out? I don't want to think about what you'd find next if you kept digging in my sister's kitchen." She gave a weak smile, but from the tone of her voice Chance could tell she was having a hard time with the thought of her sister's illicit activities.

The poor woman needed a break. He hated the thought of asking her more about Carey; Harper already had enough misery on her hands.

"Sounds great," he said, trying not to notice the way Harper's beautiful brunette hair had broken loose of the constraints of her hair tie. "It's been a long time since I took a woman on a real date."

"Date?" She jerked. "I'm not sure if we had a misunderstanding somewhere along the line here, but I'm not interested in *dating* anyone right now. I'm going back to Seattle as soon as possible."

He shouldn't have been hurt by the words that rolled from her tongue like a well-practiced line, but he couldn't help himself. Damn him and damn his ego. Of course a woman like her—strong, independent, and professional—wouldn't want to take up with a man like him. From all his time reading people, it was easy to see she wasn't interested in a man without a "real" job, a "real" income, or a "real" life. He couldn't blame her. On paper there wasn't much he could offer to a woman as far as a relationship. He was gone all the time and in his profession there was the stigma of lies and deceit.

Hell, maybe she was right in thinking she was too good for him.

"Okay. That's fine. I can just get going."

"No." She paused as if she was trying to recover from making the mistake of telling him what she really thought. He gave her a dry smile. She hadn't made a mistake. She had spoken plainly and told him exactly how she felt. There was no going back now.

"Don't misunderstand me, Chance. I want to go, but I just don't want you to think I'm looking for anything other than a friend. Let's face it, you and I are too different to make anything work—at least on any other level than friendship."

"Well, aren't you blunt?"

"I've been around."

He smirked. "You have, have you?"

"That's not what I meant." Her cheeks grew a shade pinker. "I only meant that I'm not nineteen. I'm not falling for some guy— no matter how good looking he is—just because he's standing in front of me."

His smirk turned into a full on smile—one he couldn't control. "So you think I'm good looking?"

"Dang you. I can't win, can I?" She stormed out of the bathroom, but not before he saw the smile on her lips. "Let's just go get some dinner. And no more questions."

• • •

Who did Chance Landon think he was? Just because he was handsome and had the devil's charm didn't mean she would give him any part of her heart. And if he were smart, he wouldn't give her any part of his.

So far she had missed having the men she cared about crushed by the curse of the nymphs. She had let no man fall in love with her, not even her ex-husband who she'd always held at arm's length.

It was her intention to keep any man from loving her and being struck down by a tragic death—and to stop herself from following down a path Jenna had frequented.

If nothing else, her sister had taught her what not to do and how not to live. Harper wouldn't be flippant about love. She wasn't like Jenna. She couldn't live with herself if a man died having chosen to ignore the curse just to experience love.

Chance's white cowboy hat slipped off the dashboard of the truck as he turned the wheel. He reached out and stopped the hat from falling. She couldn't help but notice the way his hair had a slight natural wave, which made his locks fall into his face like caressing fingers. His silver-tinted eyes were focused on the road as he steered his truck. The way he was so concentrated on the task at hand made it hard to not notice the way the fine lines collected around his eyes.

As much as Harper wanted to deny it, Chance Landon was handsome. Far more handsome a man than most she had met working in the lab.

She had played it brilliantly back at the house. Yes, she was absolutely attracted to him, but she had been fully justified in refusing his advance. No matter how badly her instinct driven inner-nymph would have liked to see him without a shirt—or more—she couldn't live her life that way. No.

Chance looked over at her and caught her looking. His million-dollar smile returned. "So, about Carey, did she leave you an address or anything? I was hoping to stop by her place before I head out of town."

His question jarred her back to reality; with the drugs and everything that had gone on between them she had forgotten the real reason he had come to see her. "Actually she's a tenant in an apartment building my sister owned. It's not far from here. It's on the way to Coeur d'Alene. Maybe we can stop by on the way to dinner."

"Sounds good. What's the address?"

"962 Cemetery Road." She pulled out her smart phone and tapped the screen until she found directions to the apartment complex. "Here," she said, handing him her phone.

He took a quick glance and handed it back. "I got it."

She rolled her eyes—why couldn't men take directions? "Why do you think she was looking for you, Chance? "

He shifted uncomfortably in his seat. "I have no idea what Carey wants. But I'm sorry she got you mixed up in her business."

"You don't need to apologize. It's not all bad," she said, trying to not look him in the face.

"I'm glad you feel that way. But I hope nothing happens to change your mind. I mean, you haven't seen me eat dinner yet." He gave a short laugh, but she could sense his nervousness as he tapped on the steering wheel.

"Chance, is there something you aren't telling me?"

He glanced over at her. "What do you mean? About dinner? Let's see … I'm not one for Chinese food. I'm more of a steak and potatoes guy."

That's not what she had meant and he knew it. "Are you in some kind of trouble with Carey?"

"Why would you ask me something like that?"

"Look, I don't mean anything by it, but are you afraid of Carey or something? You seem nervous. And don't tell me I'm wrong."

"You're not wrong. I've just learned that when it comes to Carey I can never expect things to go a certain way. Maybe it's not such a great idea for you to go with me there. I can't guarantee what she'll say."

"No, it's fine. I'm not worried about Carey. She seemed upset at the services, but I think it was just because she was looking for you. If anything, I think she'll be happy to know I found you."

"I like that about you—you're not afraid to face things head-on—or while tripping over barstools." He teased her with a broad smile, but his smile looked strange, almost off, like he put it there only for her.

Chance steered the truck down a winding road toward the aging beige apartment buildings Harper now owned. The siding was starting to slip, giving the building the look of a tiered cake on the verge of tipping over. The all-weather carpeting on the stairs leading up to the upper floors was worn through, exposing chipped and crumbling concrete.

From the look of the place the complex was going to be a challenge to sell. Harper's only hope was that she could sell it cheap to get out quick. After what they had found in the house, she hated to think of the mess they would find within the derelict apartments.

"There," Harper said, pointing up to the third floor apartment with the brass number *316* outside of its door. The six hung upside down, making it look like a nine. "I think that's Carey's apartment."

Chance pulled the truck into a parking spot next to a car with a flat tire.

"Do you want to go in? Or would you rather stay here?" Chance grabbed his cowboy hat off the dashboard and pushed it down over his locks, making him more irresistible than ever. When she thought about him going up to see another woman, a strange wave of jealousy passed through her.

She pushed open the door of the truck. "I'd hate to miss all the fun."

It surprised her when Chance met her at the front of the truck and took her hand, almost as if he knew she needed his support. He was warm and his palms were sweaty from nerves, but whether that caused by her or the thought of meeting up with Carey, she didn't know. She secretly hoped she could cause that reaction, but nothing had passed between them besides a few smiles.

"My ex-wife can be a bit of a handful." He ran his thumb over the back of Harper's hand, and his voice seemed quiet, but it could have been the pounding of her heart that made it difficult for her to hear. "I'm just throwing it out there, but I'm thinking that there's a connection between your sister, Carey, and the drugs we found."

"What?" Harper snapped back to reality. "Do you think they were dealing drugs together?"

"I wouldn't put it past Carey."

She couldn't deny all the trouble Jenna had caused in her life, but it still hurt to hear Chance talk about what a mess her sister had become. Harper pulled her fingers away from Chance's.

He looked disappointed as he dropped his hand to his side. "I didn't mean to upset you, I just mean it seems strange that your sister owns the building that my ex-wife lives in. Do you think it's possible your sister was dealing?"

Harper walked over to the bottom of the stairs and looked back over her shoulder. "It's hard to say what my sister was doing." She stepped up the stairs. "Let's just get this over with."

Chance made his way up the steps, taking the lead. She trudged behind, silently reprimanding herself for letting his bluntness bother her.

Making her way to the top of the third floor steps, she could hear the rap of Chance's knuckles against the apartment's door.

"Hello?" Chance stepped to the window and peered inside. "Carey? You in there?" He reached down to the door handle and, with a twist, the door swung open.

"Oh my God." Harper's hands flew over her mouth.

In the middle of the living room, spread out on the floor like a fallen bird, was the redheaded woman she had met at Jenna's funeral. Carey's face was the pale purple mottled color of death. A needle protruded from her arm.

The scent of decay wafted out of the apartment, filling Harper's nostrils. White feathers were strewn around, as if someone had torn through a pillow, filling the room with its eerie down.

On the woman's face was the terror of whatever it was she had last seen. Something about her ghostly, clouded gaze reminded her of Jenna lying in the white casket. The thought made Harper's breath catch in her throat and come out as a thin wheeze.

Chance grabbed Harper and pulled her into his arms, shielding her view. . "Harper, don't look. It's okay. It's all going to be okay."

Chapter Seven

What was Chance going to do? He couldn't leave the body for someone else to find. No matter how much he disliked Carey, she deserved more respect than for him to leave her body untended.

He loosened his embrace on Harper. Her eyes were filled with terror and disgust and he hated to let her go. She'd been through so much with losing her sister and now this, but he couldn't hold her forever, no matter how badly he desired it. "Sweetheart, I think you should go stand away from the door. You don't need to see this."

Harper answered with a tight nod as he let his embrace fall away. She turned and stepped out of the doorway. Her footsteps made a hollow sound as she walked down the walkway in the direction of the next apartment, thankfully out of sight from the macabre scene.

Covering his mouth and nose, Chance stepped into the small apartment and glanced around the space. On the walls were a few pictures all of a black-haired girl at varying ages. The last photo was of a girl who was maybe about seventeen.

Chance couldn't believe what he was seeing. There was no way Carey was dead.

Stepping next to the body, Chance did the only thing he knew—he reached down and pressed his fingers against Carey's neck. Her skin was sickeningly cold.

There was no question in his mind as he glanced around at the white feathers that filled the room. Someone had killed her by pulling her feathers when she'd been in her shift. But who had gotten close enough to attack his ex-wife? Who wanted her dead?

Taking his fingers from her neck, he touched her eyelids and pulled them closed. Out of respect he mouthed a quick prayer, but it had been so long since he'd prayed that he barely knew the right words.

• • •

The nosey neighbors stood on the walkway and around the parking lot as the coroner and his assistant lifted the body and carried it down the three flights of stairs. The whole scene made Chance's belief in people lessen. The only person who didn't seem grossly attracted to the investigation was Harper. She leaned against a wall, seemingly not noticing the black bag and its macabre contents, as a police officer continued to ask her questions.

The only reason she had been exposed to this was because of him and his curiosity. He should have never asked her to tell him where Carey lived. He should have never brought her here.

A police officer walked up to him. The officer stared at the ground, the walls, the steps, everywhere except Chance's face. The man gave a little cough as he attempted to clear his nerves. "You're Chance Landon, correct?"

"Yes."

"Sir, the investigator just let me know that we have a letter, which was left by the deceased. It looks as though she might have known her time was coming."

"What? Who was the letter addressed to?"

"It was addressed to you," the officer said.

"Can I have it?"

"First, I have a few questions that I need to ask you."

"Why? I've made it more than clear I didn't have anything to do with this," Chance said, trying to clear any ideas the officer had of making him a suspect.

"At this point, it looks like a drug overdose, but we won't know for sure until toxicology comes back—and that may take some time. However, from the state of her apartment, we do have to treat this as a crime scene since the death was not witnessed."

"I understand," Chance said, trying to be as compliant as possible. The last thing he needed was the cops on his ass for something he didn't have any part of. "How long do you think she had been here before we found her?"

"I'm not an investigator, but from the rate of rigor mortis they approximated the death to be somewhere between eight and twenty-four hours ago." The officer pushed one of his thumbs under the edge of his utility belt. "Just to cover the bases, I do have some questions for you about your whereabouts."

Chance took a step back and bumped against the railing of the walkway. "I didn't have anything to do with Carey's death."

"Sir, all I'm asking is where you were for the last twenty-four hours?" The officer seemed almost bored as he asked the required question.

Chance glanced over in Harper's direction and remembered the drugs. He couldn't very well tell them he'd been busy aiding in the disposal of narcotics. "I was with Harper. Before that I was in my hotel room with my buddy, and last night I was playing poker."

"Both of these people can account for your whereabouts?"

"Absolutely." His legs seemed to go numb as his body compensated for the shock of the officer's questioning. "I'm sure if you need, the hotel might have cameras. You'll see I never left until I went to see Harper."

"Great. Just got a couple more questions," the officer continued. "Sir, why were you here today?"

"I just stopped by."

The officer finally looked him in the face. "And how would you classify your relationship with the diseased?"

What relationship?

Chance's hands gripped the winter chilled metal railing. "She and I were married a while back. I hadn't talked to her since our divorce."

"When exactly was your divorce?"

He thought for a moment. "We signed the papers seventeen years ago, thereabouts."

"So what would you say was the reason for your divorce?"

"Irreconcilable differences."

The man gave a quick laugh. "I can certainly understand that … Me and my ex just went through one hell of a divorce."

"Sorry to hear about it," Chance said, grateful that the officer wasn't digging too deeply into his life.

"When we get involved with these kind of women," the officer said, as he motioned toward the black body bag in the coroner's hands, "it's never a good thing. Right?"

The man must have assumed Carey was just another druggie off the street, but Chance knew better—there was more going on than a simple overdose.

The cop stuffed his thumb under his utility belt and leaned back. "And what about your daughter? Do you know where we can find her?"

"I don't have a daughter."

The officer jerked and there was a flicker of confusion on his face. He pressed a button on the walkie-talkie clipped to his chest and turning, walked a few steps away. Chance tried to hear what the officer said, but he could only make out muffled whispers.

After a moment the officer turned back around and walked to him. "Sir, along with the letter left by the deceased was a birth certificate for one Starling Jackson."

"And?"

"And you were named as the father of the girl."

What was going on? Carey, as a nymph, couldn't have gotten pregnant, could she?

"There's no way."

"Legally, sir, you are the girl's father. We called her school, but they said she is already out for the day. She's probably on her way home now."

"Child? How old is she?"

"The certificate date shows she, Starling Jackson, is seventeen." And then Chance remembered. The week the divorce had been finalized, he and Carey had run into each other in a smoke-filled bar. After one too many beers for him, and more than one or two too many cocktails for her, they had gone back to her place. Had their one last fling resulted in a child?

The knot in his stomach tightened. Was the child the reason Carey had been trying to contact him? It wasn't beneath her to want to keep a child a secret from him. If she had told him about his daughter, she would have known he would have wanted to have parental rights.

He hadn't hated her, but in that moment his feelings changed. Any woman who could deceive this much—a woman who could keep his child a secret from him, deserved his hatred.

"Sir? Are you okay?" the officer asked.

Was the guy kidding? He just learned he had a child. No. Not just a child, but a teenage daughter. It didn't seem real.

"Yeah."

"Here's the letter and your daughter's birth certificate." The officer handed him an envelope.

Chance took the envelope. On the outside, in Carey's familiar handwriting, was his name. He pulled out the first paper. On the top of the birth certificate was Starling's name and then Carey's information. Further down the page was he was listed as the father.

Even though Carey had problems, she wouldn't have listed him if he hadn't been the girl's father. However, it surprised him that she wouldn't have merely left the father's information blank. Was it possible that her naming him was a safeguard in the event something happened—something like him finding her dead?

He folded the certificate and carefully slid it back into the envelope and withdrew the letter. He was surprised to see Carey had only written him three words—three agonizing words—Chance, I'm sorry.

The officer stared at him.

"Are you willing to take the child, or would you rather we put her in foster care when she arrives?"

"No." Chance tensed. "I'll take her."

"Great. We hate to see children taken from the biological parents in cases like these."

Harper excused herself from the officer she was talking to and made her way toward him.

"Chance, you look terrible. Are you okay?"

"I have a child. A teenager. Starling." He blurted the words out. Her eyes widened and her face paled.

"What are you talking about? She couldn't have had a child, Carey was a—"

"Was a what?" the officer interrupted.

Harper's gaze snapped to the officer. "She was always a surprise." She gave an unconvincing laugh.

The officer stared at her. "How well did you know the deceased?"

Harper gave the officer a melting smile. "Officer, I already gave my statement to your friend over there." She pointed at the secondary officer. "I'm just such a mess, would you mind terribly if you talked to him about it?"

A strange wave of energy passed by Chance, almost like a warm summer wind. The officer flipped his notepad shut and returned the beautiful woman's smile. "Not a problem, thanks for being so open to questioning. I know this must be hard on you, ma'am."

Harper fluttered her eyelashes and the strange energy intensified. His body warmed with the same sensation he used to feel when he'd first met Carey. It had been seventeen years since he had felt that, seventeen years since he'd been around a woman like Carey—a woman who was a nymph.

Chapter Eight

How could Carey possibly have gotten pregnant? It had been almost a century since the last nymph had been born, so it wasn't completely impossible, but it seemed unlikely. And if Carey had birthed a child, how hadn't the news spread through the sisterhood? Harper had more questions than answers, but one question rose above the rest: How much did Chance Landon know?

He had to have some idea that his ex-wife was a nymph. Or maybe not.

The gray sky was ominous, like a smothering pillow above them. The gray perfectly matched Chance's face. He hadn't known he had a daughter and, if Carey had chosen to not disclose her daughter's life, it seemed unlikely she would tell him something as challenging as the fact that she was a nymph—not only a nymph, but one who had been cursed.

What man would stay around after he found out he would die if the woman fell in love? It was easy to understand why Carey would leave out the bits about her supernatural abilities and her curse. Harper was no different—she'd never told a human what or who she was—and she wasn't about to start.

There was a slam of a door as the last of the officers got in their patrol car to leave. It had been a long day and something told her it was far from being over.

"What are you going to do about Starling, Chance?"

"I don't know … " He shook his head as if he was in a daze.

She couldn't imagine what he was going through. It was a lot just to find out that someone you cared for had died. To add the fact that Carey had a child—and not just a child, but his child—was news that would change his life in countless ways. From the stunned look on his face, Harper could see he was thinking the same thing.

"I'm sorry Carey kept her a secret from you. You had the right to know."

"Apparently she didn't think I needed to know about Starling." A deep sadness filled his voice.

She wanted to take him into her arms, to hold him and tell him everything would be okay, just as he had done for her when they'd found Carey. Yet she couldn't. She couldn't lie to him.

"Well, Carey was wrong."

He leaned back against the railing and crossed his arms over his chest. "No, she wasn't."

"What do you mean?"

"I'm no saint, Harper. Carey had every right to keep the truth and the girl away from me." He dropped his gaze to the ground. "I chose to leave Carey and get a divorce. I could have given up my life as a professional poker player, but I didn't. I left. I'm sure she thought I didn't deserve to have a relationship with Starling."

"Starling is your daughter. Regardless of what you think you did, you should have known she existed."

"You say that, but you don't know anything about me."

His words ripped at Harper like a shark its prey, but she forced herself to ignore the pain. He was hurting and angry—Chance was only lashing out and she was the closest available target. "And you don't know anything about me, but that doesn't mean we can't learn—that we can't help each other. I don't know about you, but without Jenna, I don't have anyone. I could use a friend."

"I'd love to be your friend, but I need you to know that I can't offer you anything else. I'm too fucked up right now."

"Chance, I wasn't offering anything to you besides a friendship."

The space between them filled with an awkward silence. In a way, she envied his ability to push others away. If she could only be as distant as Chance, she would never have to face getting hurt.

"That's good, because I need a friend who can help me. I don't know anything about how to raise a teenage girl." Chance paused.

"And the police told me that I have primary custody of Starling." His eyes seemed to absorb the gray of the clouds—or it could have been the gray of his soul desperately trying to escape. "They told me if I don't take her she will be taken into the foster care system. And there's no way I would let my child grow up being shuffled from one hell to another. She's almost eighteen, but no child deserves to be lost to a broken system."

"You're right, and I'm here—you can always call me for whatever you need."

"First thing, I think I need to find Starling. The cop said she was off from school." He glanced down at his watch. "She should've been back here by now. We need to find her."

There was a squeak of a rusty hinge as a door opened. An ashy blonde with dark bags under her eyes and scabs across her cheeks looked out from her apartment. "What in the hell's going on out here? First the cops, and now you guys won't shut the fuck up." Her sunken cheeks pulled against her jaw as she forced her words out like a hardcore drug addict.

"Sorry," Chance said, as he took a step toward the stairs. "We're just about to go."

"No, wait." Harper motioned for him to stop. "Ma'am, have you by chance seen a young girl? Black hair? About seventeen? Her name's Starling?"

The woman stepped out of her doorway, but shrugged. "Like I told those motherfucking cops, there are a lot of brats running around here. Can't say whether I did or not."

"We're no cops. We're just looking for my daughter." Chance took the lead.

"If you ain't no cop, maybe we can come to an arrangement." The pock-marked woman rubbed her fingers together and gestured toward Chance's back pocket.

From the look of the woman and this derelict place, Harper hated to think what the money would go toward buying, but they needed to find Starling and the meth head was their only hope. "My purse is in the truck. Do you have any cash?"

Chance pulled out his wallet and took out a few bills. Before he fully extended his arm, the woman grabbed the money and stuffed it into the waistband of her baggy gray sweatpants.

"What'd ya say she looked like?" The neighbor wiped her arm under her nose.

"Wait, there's a picture in the apartment. Let me get it." Harper hurried back to the apartment and stepped through the yellow tape.

Careful to step around the mark on the floor where Carey's body had rested, Harper grabbed the photo off the wall and flipped it over. On the back of the cheap cardboard-backed frame it read, *To Mom—Happy Mother's Day. Love, Starling.* The note was written in tight jagged letters, far different from the looping, lazy letters that a normal seventeen-year-old girl would write.

She pulled the picture out of the frame and hung the empty frame back on the wall. As she turned, Harper couldn't stop herself from staring at the sickening spot on the floor. One lazy fly buzzed down from the ceiling so slowly it looked like it was moving in the haze of a bad dream. The insect landed where Carey's head had rested.

It haunted Harper how, just like Jenna, Carey could leave this world with more questions than answers.

Slipping the door shut, Harper hurried back to Chance and the meth addict. Chance looked relieved to see her return. The woman had an ugly sneer on her pockmarked face. "What were you doing in there, baking fucking cookies, Betty Crocker?"

Harper couldn't bear the thought of a child living near such a vile woman. "Here," she said handing the woman the picture. "This is her, Starling Jackson."

The woman drew her fingers to her face and picked at one of the scabs on her chin until blood started to ooze from under her fingernail. "Yeah, I seen this girl."

"When?" Chance jerked as he finally got the answer they both needed.

"I dunno. She wanders around here a lot, but never says much."

"Do you know where we can find her?" Chance pressed.

The woman smiled as if she enjoyed holding all the power for once in her life. "I think so, but it's gonna cost you. I got kids to feed of my own." She pointed back at her apartment, as the sound of televised gunshots and actors yelling rattled out into the late evening air.

Chance pulled a few more bills from his wallet. The woman took them greedily and this time stuffed the money down her stained white shirt, revealing a dirty red bra. "She likes to hang out down at the end of this hall. I see her goin' into the last apartment all the time." She jabbed her blood-covered thumb toward an apartment where a tin coffee can, overflowing with cigarette butts, sat next to a threadbare recliner.

A pit opened up in Harper's stomach as she thought of all the possibilities of what the girl might have been doing in that apartment.

"Thanks," Chance said. He took the picture from the woman and, folding it, put it into his wallet.

"Yeah," the woman grunted as she stepped back into her apartment. The door slammed shut and the woman yelled from the other side.

"Well, she was helpful," Harper whispered, even though the yelling woman couldn't have possibly heard.

Chance gave her a weak, half upturned smile as he slid his wallet back into his pocket. "At least it was a start. We need to find Starling, no matter how much it costs."

She couldn't agree more. The girl needed out of this place—she needed to live somewhere safe.

Chance led the way past door after door until they came to the end of the hall where they had to step around the dingy chair. Burn holes covered the armrest and an orange cap, which Harper recognized as a needle cover, was stuffed into a crack in the cushion.

The door was missing its knob, so Chance had to hold it closed as he rapped his knuckles against its smudged surface.

"Hello, anybody there?" Chance called.

No answer. Chance looked back at her and shrugged.

"Let's go in."

"You stay out here. I don't know what we're going to find," Chance said with a look of pity upon his face.

"I'm fine," Harper lied. "Besides, I'm sure your daughter is alright."

Chance cringed as she said the words *your daughter*.

She stepped past him and put her hand on his. "Why don't we go in together?"

Her fingers lingered on his rough skin and the warmth of his flesh seeped into hers. He looked at her, and stared into her eyes. "Thank you, Harper. And I'm sorry for dragging you into this mess. I know what you're going through. You didn't deserve to have to deal with this too."

Her heart shifted. "Chance, I'm glad I'm here. I know what it's like to be alone and having to deal with everything life throws at you."

She moved to open the door and her body brushed against his arm, but their gaze never wavered from one another. His stormy eyes seemed to warm. He was so close she could smell his rich, manly scent. The heat of his breath brushed against her cheek like a wanting hand.

Chance leaned in and, in one smooth motion, took her lips with his own. His full lips pressed against hers and she nipped at his bottom lip, giving him a sexy reminder he was playing a dangerous game. His body tensed against her arm and he leaned back.

"Damn it." He stepped away. "I shouldn't have done that."

He was right, but she couldn't regret his stealing the moment. "You're right," she answered, trying to catch her breath.

His brows furrowed and for a split second he looked upset that she would agree with him. "Let's go."

The door opened and the smell of sour milk and mouse droppings wafted out, forcing Harper to cover her nose. There, sitting in the center of the room, sat a young girl. Her black hair was disheveled, as if it had been days since it had last seen a brush.

"Starling?" Chance asked.

The girl didn't look up.

Harper stepped by him, careful not to touch him again. "Sweetheart?" She stepped next to the girl and kneeled down, getting at her level. "Starling?"

Harper reached out and touched the girl's shoulder. The girl jerked and looked up at Harper with piercing sea blue eyes. There was a look of fear on her face, as if until this moment she had not been aware of anyone around her. "Who? Who're you?"

Chance stepped next to them and, moving a dirty shirt out of the way, he knelt down. "Are you Starling Jackson?"

The young girl nodded, but looked back down at the pad of paper and pencil in her lap, which was covered with strange circles and markings. She glanced back up.

"Starling, I'm your father. My name's Chance Landon."

The girl shrugged, almost unemotionally, as she stared at Chance. "Carey said you'd come if something happened to her."

"How do you know something happened to your mother?"

Starling blinked like she was numb. "I got home from school and I saw the police. I came in here to hide. Mom's dead, isn't she?"

Chance nodded, as if he couldn't say the words to the wild young woman staring up at him like a young fawn.

"Starling," Chance said with a soft edge to his deep baritone, "you're going to need to come with me and my friend Harper. We need to get you out of here."

Chapter Nine

Harper kept surprising Chance with her kindness. She was going through so much, yet she had insisted they come back to her sister's home to stay until he could decide his next step. In truth, he appreciated her offer more than she could know. It seemed better to stay at Jenna's house it was a far better place than some seedy motel. Even though Starling was his daughter, they barely knew each other.

Harper and Starling sat at the kitchen table around bags of fast food. Even though they'd spent more than three hours together, Starling had barely spoken since they'd loaded her, a suitcase, and a backpack into his pickup.

"Are you done eating?" Chance asked her.

Starling stared up at the ceiling, watching something that only she could see. There was something about Starling that was different, but Chance couldn't put his finger on exactly what was amiss. There was just something about the way she seemed to be lost in a world of her own.

Harper tapped her shoulder. "Did you hear your dad, sweetheart?"

The girl seemed to snap back to reality. "Huh?"

"Are you done eating?" Harper smiled.

Starling nodded, but looked back up at the ceiling.

Harper picked up the garbage and threw it into the bin under the kitchen sink. "If you're done, why don't I show you to your room? I bet you're exhausted."

The girl gave her a weak nod and stood up. She clasped her hands like a prim schoolgirl, a far contrast to the pale, wild looking young woman who stood before him.

Harper walked out of the kitchen and motioned for them to follow. She made her way upstairs and stepped into the guest bedroom at the far end of the hall. "There's a restroom right here," she said, pointing to the next doorway. "In there, you'll find everything you need for a bath if you want one, but the shower is acting up."

Sterling walked into the bedroom. She flopped down on the bed and pulled her worn notebook out of her backpack. "How long am I staying here?" Her question sounded like an accusation, and it made Chance wonder if she'd moved around a lot as a child. The gaping hole in his heart grew larger.

"I don't know," Harper said as he stepped next to her. "But you and your dad are welcome to stay as long as necessary."

"Thank you, Harper," he said.

"Absolutely." Harper stepped out of the bedroom. "And Starling, your dad will be staying right next door. If you need anything, don't be afraid to let one of us know, okay?"

Starling nodded, but didn't look up from the notebook that rested in her lap.

Chance pulled the door shut. "I mean it, thanks, Harper."

"You're welcome." She smiled. "It's the least I could do. I feel like this is my fault. I should've asked Carey more questions. Maybe I could've stopped this all from happening."

"I doubt it. Carey was always a loose cannon. It was only a matter of time until she wound up in trouble." Trouble always seemed to go hand-in-hand with nymphs.

Harper pushed a wayward hair out of her face. As she made her way down the stairs, a faint light made her dark hair sparkle like strands of fine copper. She was so beautiful. In fact, she was almost too beautiful.

"Harper, are you—" He stopped himself from asking her if she was a nymph. Even if she was one, he wasn't sure he wanted to know.

"Am I what?" Harper asked.

He stared at her hair where it caressed her neck. He could find out if she was a nymph now if he wanted, all he had to do was flip back her hair, and look to see if she bore the mark. If she did, he had his answer. He would know whether or not she was a nymph, just like Carey.

He reached up, but stopped himself again. What if she was a nymph? Did he really want to know? Did he really want to get involved with another cursed woman? If his relationship with Carey had taught him anything it was to steer clear of nymphs—well, as much as he could. With Starling in his life, there would be no more avoiding their kind.

Harper, misjudging his outstretched hand, took his hand in hers.

Starling footsteps echoed down from the bedroom above. "Do you think Starling is going to be alright?" he asked, avoiding her question.

"She just lost her mom and her home. Just because she isn't talkative, it doesn't mean things are always going to be this hard. She'll come through this and so will you."

"I know," he lied. It was almost unimaginable for life to get anything but harder now that he had another person to take care of. He could hardly take care of himself, let alone drag a poor young woman on the road with him.

Harper led him to the living room and sat down on the couch. Letting go of her hand, he sat down in the recliner.

"What do you think you are going to do with her?" Harper asked, leaning back on the couch.

"I don't know." He perched on the edge of the chair. "Kodie's playing in Worley tonight, but tomorrow we were going to head out to Vegas for a poker tournament. He's gonna go ape shit when he finds out about Carey's death and Starling."

"So you're going to leave?"

"We were planning on going, but now I don't know." He watched the light shift in her eyes. "I can't take Starling with me."

"Are you saying you want to leave her here with me?"

"No. No. No." He shook his head. "That's not what I was saying at all."

"Then what are you saying?"

He paused for a second as he tried to get back control of his mouth and his thoughts. There was no one, and nowhere else the girl could go except with him and Kodie.

"I'm just tired. I need to think through everything. If you don't mind, I'm going to go to bed." There were so many questions running through his mind, he barely knew where to begin to get his life, and now the life of his daughter, back in order.

•••

No matter how hard she tried, Harper couldn't fall asleep. Her heart and her mind were at an impasse. She needed to get back to Seattle, back to work, and back to her everyday life. Yet her heart wasn't letting her go—she wanted to stay here. She needed to find out if Carey's death had something to do with Jenna. And more importantly, she needed to know that Starling and Chance would be okay. The nymph needed help. She was so young. She would have more and more questions the older she became. Her battle with being a nymph was only beginning.

Harper's thoughts wandered to when she had been as young as Starling. It had been many millennia since she'd first begun to learn about her abilities—and her limitations. At first it had been fun, having the ability to seduce and control men with simply a smile, but as she had slowly aged over the centuries the fun withered away along with her youth.

She and Jenna had spent many nights making love with men they met upon the roads as they travelled, but the fertile place in

Harper's heart where love was supposed to be tended had never been sown. And it never could be. And as the realization that she could never really love grew, the loneliness in Harper's heart grew as well.

It pained Harper to think of the hard lessons that Starling would soon have to face as a budding nymph.

Maybe she could help. But to help would mean she would have to tell Starling and Chance the truth of her being. She wanted to open up to him, to tell him the truth, but she wasn't so naïve that she didn't understand such things had emotional consequences—and she was already too involved in his personal life. Plus, if Chance didn't know Carey had been a nymph, he may not know Starling was like her mother. She shuddered at the thought of not only outing herself, but Starling as well. She couldn't expose the girl.

She rolled over and touched her cell phone. Its light cast long secret filled shadows. 2:00 A.M. She sat up and flicked on the small lamp on the bedside table as she tried to rid the room of the eerie darkness. There was no point in trying to sleep. There was too much going on in her head.

There was a tap on her door, making her jerk with surprise.

For a moment she considered not answering, but there was no faking she was asleep. Whoever was standing outside of the door must have seen the light go on. They had to know she was awake.

"Who is it?" Her voice was hoarse from her tiredness.

"It's me," Chance answered.

The deep tone of his voice made her heart jerk as if the bass of his words were her favorite song. What did he want?

She smoothed the long strands of her hair. "Come in."

The door cracked open and Chance stuck his head in. "I wanted to ask you something and I saw a light on. You okay?"

"Yeah, I'm fine. Just having a hard time going to sleep."

Chance stepped into the bedroom and sat down in the small recliner in the corner. "That seems to be going around."

"Did you check on Starling?"

"Yeah, she's the only one of us who seems to be getting any shut eye."

Harper gave a weak smile. The girl had been through so much in one day, at least she could rest. "What's up? What do you need?"

Chance wrung his hands together. "Well, I'm thinking I'm going to need to hit the road in the morning. Kodie's chomping at the bit to get moving."

Her stomach dropped in disappointment. "Why? I mean you guys are more than welcome to stay here as long as you need. I'm sure you probably need to talk to her school—there's so much you need to handle."

"I don't want to be in your way, Harper. I know you have a lot going on in your life."

Harper pushed her feet out from under the covers. Chance was absolutely right. She did need to get Jenna's affairs handled, but she didn't want him to go—at least not yet. She wanted to pretend just a little bit longer that she wasn't the spinster she had become. Her fingers curled around the soft sheet as she looked at Chance. "Tell me the truth. Why are you really going? There'll be more tournaments. Don't you think it's best for Starling to stay here? Or are you leaving because of me?"

Chance looked up from his hands and sucked in a long breath. "Do you mind if I come closer?"

She did mind. If he was going to break her heart he could do it from across the room. "Fine."

He stood up and she noticed he still had his clothes on from the day before. Chance sat down on the bed across from her, close enough to touch, but a lifetime away.

"I don't have much of a choice, Harper. I have to go."

"What do you mean? Everyone has a choice." She let her fingers uncurl from the edge of the sheet as she turned to face him.

"No, I made a promise to help Kodie out. He borrowed some money from a guy and the time is coming when he's going to need to pay him back."

"You agreed to back a loan for another poker player?" Chance seemed to be so intelligent, and he seemed to have his head on straight, so what had he been thinking vouching for the man?

"Kodie and I've known each other a long time. He was having a bad night in Vegas a few months back and he went to Three-Eyed Nate when he was desperate."

"You let him borrow money from a man named Three-Eyed Nate?"

"It was stupid. He'd already taken the loan before I knew what was going on, or I would've never allowed it. He already owed me some money and I think he was afraid to come back to me for more."

"As much as I don't agree with the position Kodie put you in, I think it's nice you would have your friend's back. There aren't many people in the world who would go that far for a friend."

"Kodie's been there for me during some really rough patches. The least I can do is be there for him. It's what a real man does for his friend."

Harper stared down at his fingers resting almost exactly at the center of the full-sized bed. "So you're really going in the morning?"

"You sound relieved."

In a way she was relieved. There would be no more emotional turmoil if he left, she could avoid the anxiety she felt when he was near. She could go back to a life where most things were controlled and fit into her nice little routine. Chance was far too spontaneous, far too impulsive to fit into her life. He was everything she wasn't—even his smile was uncontrollable ... and he was heart-wrenchingly handsome. "Not relieved exactly," she answered. "I'm only wondering if I should go buy more groceries. I don't want Starling to find anything in the freezer that we wouldn't want her to find."

Chance gave a half laugh. "It's funny how we keep finding things we don't want to find."

"And how the things I'm looking for I can't seem to find."

"And what are you looking for exactly?"

Harper's cheeks warmed for a second as she realized what he was implying. "There are a lot of things, but sometimes we can't have the things we search for."

Harper let her fingers move a little bit closer to his. Maybe, just maybe she could let her nymphish desires run free and she could have one night of passion-filled bliss before they both went their separate ways.

"Sometimes what we are not searching for is the thing we find," Chance said as he reached over and his fingers found hers.

"I also need to find some books ... for Starling," she said slowly, more than aware that she didn't care about the words she was forming with her lips. All she cared about was the warm touch of Chance's hand against hers, and the need for more. "I made a promise."

He lifted her hand to his lips. "Promises are something I can't give you." His warm breath caressed her hand. "But I can tell you I'll try to make you happy for tonight."

She should have said no or stopped him from brushing his full lips over the thin skin on the back of her hand, but her body wouldn't allow her thoughts to escape as words. Her body wanted this, no, her body *needed* this. She was a nymph, the seductress, the demigod of carnal desires—and she could think of no one she wanted more than the man who shared her bed. Everything else in the world could wait. For one night, and only this one night, she would allow her inner demigod to be free and to follow the needs of her body and her heart.

Chance pulled her hand lightly and drew her across the bed and into his lap. His full lips met hers in an explosive combination of lust and excitement and she was overtaken with a deep need to possess all of him. But it could wait. If they only had this one night together, this one stolen night in a lifetime of noes, then she was going to enjoy every fleeting moment. She slowed their kiss, letting his moist lips caress the soft folds of her own until a moan threatened to escape.

She tilted her head back as if the moan would slip back down her throat, but Chance took the opportunity and languished in her blissful agony as he trailed the tip of his tongue down the line of her neck.

He stopped at the little dip at the base of her throat and lavished her with kisses. "This place is mine." His voice was hoarse and raspy, echoing her desire. "We only have tonight, this one night together before I leave, but I want no man to ever own this place again."

It surprised her that he would be the type who would want to own a place on her body, but she could understand his need to savor this moment forever. She ran her finger down the edge of his ear, stopping at the place where his earlobe connected with his neck. Sitting up in his lap, she touched his soft skin with her kiss-dampened lips. "Okay, but this place is mine," she whispered into his ear, making his body quiver.

He turned his head, forcing her lips from the soft flesh of his ear, and his warm breath brushed against her cheek again. His eyes closed and opened and their eyes met. For the first time, she noted his eyes weren't just silver. No, instead they carried the brilliance of finely buffed platinum. Chance reached up and ran his rough finger over the tender curves of her lip, drawing chills to her skin.

"You're an amazing woman, has anyone ever told you?"

She smiled, letting his thumb slip from her lip. "Only you." She bent her head down and took his thumb into her mouth, careful to not look away from his eyes.

He sucked in a rattling breath. "Harper," he moaned.

"Hmm?" she answered, refusing to break the soft suction she'd created on his finger.

"Are you sure you want to do this?"

She stopped and released his thumb. "What do you mean? You don't want this? You don't want me?"

His lust-filled gaze lightened. "That's not what I'm saying. I just want to make sure we are on the same page."

He hadn't needed to speak the words that he didn't want a relationship. He wasn't alone in the sentiment.

Slipping out of his lap, she dropped onto her knees and took the waist of his jeans in her hands. She smiled up at him, refusing to acknowledge what he had said. "Lay back."

Chance's eyes closed; his endorphins must have kicked in, giving him a look of near euphoria. He dropped to his elbows as he leaned back on the baby pink satin bedspread. She ran her fingers under the edge of his pants, toward the top button. She stopped. The button was already undone. "What's this? Were you hoping I'd sleep with you?" She laughed.

"No." He reached down with his right hand and moved to close the wayward button, but she stopped him. "But I have to admit I sleep naked. And when I saw your light was on, I had to slip my pants back on to come talk to you. I guess I forgot to button."

"So you're saying you're not wearing any underwear?" She gave him a wicked smile.

Chance's laughter filled the small room.

"Shhh ... " She put her finger to her lip. "Starling's sleeping. We don't want to wake her."

His laughter quieted.

"You're a dirty man." She pushed his hand back down to the bed and went back to his open button. "But at least there's less to throw on the floor."

"Yes," he said, tilting his head back as she slid his zipper open, revealing a patch of soft brown hair. "We … we wouldn't want a mess."

Harper stood up and pulled off his pants, careful not to let them rub too hard against him. She let them fall to the floor with a soft thud and dropped back down to her knees.

His legs were covered with fine hair a shade lighter than the hair at the intersection of his thighs. She grazed her finger up his legs, starting at his ankle, moving to his knees, and ever so slowly twisting her fingers up the fine hairs toward his waiting member. He was larger than she had imagined; he would leave her well-satisfied.

He sucked in a breath, his body stiffening under her fingers as she bent down and took him into her mouth. His body shifted and he dropped to his back. Reaching down, he pushed her hair back and down her neck, exposing her face.

His body shuddered as she looked up and caught his gaze as she ran her tongue up his length.

"Come here," he said in a ragged breath. "I want you on top."

Letting go of him, she stood up.

"First," he said, sitting up on his elbows, "take off your shirt for me."

His command was playful, but the way he took control made the dampness between her thighs increase. Fingers trembling, she reached down and lifted the hem of her soft satin camisole and inched it upward, exposing the gentle curvature of her belly.

He reached up and ran his hand up under her shirt. His fingers found her sensitive nipples and he gently ran his rough thumbs over her tender flesh, making her skin prickle with excitement. He pushed up her shirt, exposing her naked breasts, and took her nipple into his mouth. His tongue flicked against her nubs and he let go. His hands slid up and she twisted out of her shirt and let him throw it to the ground.

Chance smiled as he traced his fingers down her sides and took in the sight of her body. His hands stopped at her pajama pants. Leaning in, he dropped his head on her soft underbelly. "I've wanted this since the first moment I met you."

She ran her fingers through his long locks, twisting his soft hair between her fingers. "I've wanted this too."

He pulled at her pants, slipping them down her thighs, exposing her to the night-chilled air. She stepped forward, letting the pants fall free of her skin.

"My God, you're breathtaking," Chance said, his breath catching in his throat.

If only he knew the truth, that the reason she was so beautiful was because of her lineage, her demigod line. She was made to seduce, to make men want her, to marvel in her beauty. Yet, he could never know. He could never be exposed to the danger of the truth.

She forced her thoughts from her mind. This was her one night of unbridled freedom, the freedom to follow her heart, to follow her desire, and delve into the depths of euphoria.

Chapter Ten

Chance wrapped his arms around Harper as she laid her head on his chest. His heart thumped, marking the seconds as they slipped by in their constant race with life. Harper looked up and gave him a well-pleasured and tired smile. She dropped her head back down. In the faint light given off from the bedside lamp, the streaks of copper in her hair danced.

Lifting a lock of her hair, he moved it away from her neck, exposing a black tattoo just below where her neck connected with her shoulders. He moved so he could better see the small image. He sucked in a breath as he noticed the beautiful black swan—just like Carey's.

Harper's locks fell from his fingers and landed on her bare flesh like loving fingers. If she was a nymph, those fingerlike hairs were the key to her survival. Yet, she let him touch her hair like she was any other woman—which meant she must have trusted him with her life.

Her trust made the trickle of guilt in his gut turn into a raging current. Should he tell her he held a secret of his own—one that matched the intensity and surrealism of her supernatural nature?

He drew his finger over the blackened lines of the swan. "How well did you know Carey?"

"Hmmm," Harper said, still exhausted by their lovemaking. "I just met her, I told you."

"There was no other connection between you, I mean besides Jenna?" He pressed the issue, hoping she would open up.

Harper looked up from his chest and his fingers fell from her. "Don't you believe me?"

He hadn't meant for her to think he was questioning her honesty—he simply wanted the real answers. The truth that all supernaturals would hide from the human world.

"I do believe you. That's not what I meant."

She eyed him suspiciously. "Then what do you mean?"

"Nothing."

He couldn't outright ask her if she was a nymph. If she wasn't, she would think he had lost his mind, and there would be no way he could explain his suspicions—not without revealing his own truth. Yet, if she was a nymph there would be a world of possibilities, laid out before them—and also a new set of vulnerabilities and weaknesses.

Harper dropped her head back down, but this time her body was rigid and tense in his arms.

"Harper?" he asked in a soft voice barely above a whisper. "Is there anything about you I should know?"

She jerked in his arms and sat upright. Her tell was obvious—he had been a poker player for too many years not to notice the way her gaze flashed around the room like she was looking for an escape—a classic fight or flight maneuver that always gave away someone who was trying to conceal something.

"What?" she asked as she glanced at the door.

"You can be honest with me. If there is anything you need to tell me, I won't judge. I'll accept anything you have to tell me. Anything."

There was a look of confusion on her face. "What are you after?"

He thought for a second. "Have you ever been in the hospital before?"

Harper nibbled on her lip. "No."

"How old are you? Really?"

She glanced back at the door. "Twenty-nine."

Though she looked twenty-nine her tell had once again given her lie away.

"Then who was the tenth president of the United States?

She thought for a second. "John Tyler."

He couldn't control the smile that took over his face. "Do you really expect me to believe that a *regular* person would know some random detail like that? I bet there are only a handful of humans who could name the tenth president off the top of their head."

"What do you mean, Chance?" Harper's face pinched into a tight scowl. "You don't know me. How do you know I'm not some history buff?"

"I didn't see a single history book."

"That's my sister's house—not mine."

"I know, but something tells me you and your sister had a few of the same interests. And I think Carey might have had the same interests as well—interests that involve the swan on your back."

"What? What are you talking about?" she stammered.

"Harper … " He paused as he decided how to proceed. "Are you a nymph?"

Her face flushed and she jumped out of bed. "Carey told you?"

He couldn't help but stare at her beautiful, unmarred flesh—skin too perfect to be that of a regular human woman. "Are you admitting you are one?"

Harper stared at him, as if she was trying to decide whether to fly free of the confines of the room or to stay and face his questioning. She reached out and her fingers brushed against the blanket as if she was going to take the cloth and cover her body. Before she could pull the blanket from the bed, he took her fingers in his and stopped her—she didn't need to run. He wasn't trying to hurt her. No. He only wanted to know the truth.

"You can tell me, Harper." He tried to soften the admission. "We all have secrets. If this is yours, I want you to know you can trust me."

Harper stood still, staring down at their entwined fingers. After a moment she reached up with her left hand and laid it on top. She gripped their hands as if she wanted to meld their flesh together, to make them one being—with a shared heart.

"So you knew Carey was a nymph?" She looked up.

Her soft caramel-colored eyes were laced with fear and it made the knot of nerves in his stomach clench tighter. "Yes. She told me."

"Why? Why did she tell?"

"Before we were married, she wanted to tell me everything about who she was. She respected me enough to tell me the truth of your kind—and your curse."

Harper sat down on the edge of the bed. Her simple action made the knot in his stomach loosen.

"Chance," she said softly, letting go of their entwined hands. "I have to say I don't understand. I don't understand why she would tell you … or why she would put you in that kind of danger. It's … she … acted so selfishly. Don't you think if she cared for you at all that she would have wanted to protect you from such a terrible curse?" She dropped her hand to the bed, steadying her body.

Of course Harper would never think there was anything to the story besides Carey being selfish and reckless.

"She did try to protect me."

"Even with Starling?" she asked softly, as if the words weren't an accusation, rather a way to draw his attention to what really mattered.

"I'm not sure what she was trying to do by not telling me about Starling, but I'm sure she had her reasons."

"Do you think she didn't tell you about Starling because Starling is a nymph?"

"I'm not sure she is a nymph. I can't just come out and ask her. She barely knows me," Chance said. "But maybe she'll tell me when she's ready. At least I hope so."

"That still doesn't make sense as to why Carey wouldn't have told you about your child."

"As many problems as Carey had, she wasn't all bad. There was a time when she was great. Times when her only goal in life was to be happy—and maybe she thought by not telling me she could get back to being happy."

"Being happy doesn't always mean you are making the right choice. Sometimes you have to think about other people before yourself."

"Harper, she was aware of the consequences of her curse—and she wanted to protect me, but she didn't need to ... There's something about me you don't know."

Her fingers slipped from the sheets and she turned and exposed all of her beautiful form. She deserved to know the truth, especially since he knew the truth about her. And who knew, maybe they could make this more than a one night thing, but in order for anything to happen they needed to stand on even ground.

"What don't I know?"

There was no going back. "I'm ... like you."

"You mean a shifter?"

He shook his head. "No ... not a shifter. I'm a demigod. My mother was human and my father was a god."

He half expected her to run from the room, but Harper sat still as she must have been thinking about his revelation.

"It's been a long time since I've met a demigod."

He exhaled a breath he hadn't known he'd been holding.

"If you're a demigod," Harper paused, "does that mean Zeus's curse doesn't affect you?"

"I'm not completely immortal. I'm like you, harder to kill than a mere human, but given the chance to live as an immortal. As for Zeus's curse ... " He shrugged. "I'm still here. I loved Carey, but I don't know if she felt the same. It's hard to say exactly what effect the curse has on a demigod, but I'm not gonna worry about what could happen."

The air buzzed with unspoken concerns. From the troubled look upon Harper's beautiful face, it was easy to see that she didn't agree. "You probably don't really want to hear about my relationship with Carey, but the truth is that she was worried about the curse too. We took one day at a time. We loved each other, but there was always a wall."

Chance tried to not stare at the tender skin of Harper's thighs and think of running his fingers up that skin to make her forget their troubles. "Carey would never admit that she was running from some of her feelings. And I never blamed her. She couldn't let herself love when all she knew that I could be killed anytime for our love."

"You don't need to explain the way Carey felt to me," Harper said softly. "I know how a nymph must guard her heart out of the fear of losing the person she cares about."

"Sometimes running away is the only answer." *But it didn't make the pain any less intense.* "Who is your father?" Harper asked, clearly trying to change the subject.

"My father was the god Caerus, the youngest child of Zeus."

"Your father's the god of luck? No wonder you're a gambler."

"There's a lot more to being a good gambler besides just being lucky. You have to be smart and know when you should take a bet or walk away. And more than anything, you need to know when to take a chance."

Chapter Eleven

Chance had slipped out of her bedroom in the night, making an excuse of Starling in the house as a need to hide their night of passion. He was right, but her arms had never felt emptier. For a moment, Harper wondered if she had made a mistake in allowing her body to overtake her mind, but then she thought of the secrets they shared and the new and overwhelming connection they had made. They had shared things about themselves that few were privy to—there was no going back to an in-the-box friendship. They had moved into a new realm of a relationship—more than friends, sharing lovers, but, each for their own reasons, still unable to love.

Chance had talked about being a good gambler and knowing it was more than luck. Sometimes being good was knowing what bet to take and when to walk away. For Harper, this was one of those moments in life when she needed to look to the lessons and pain of her past. If she had learned anything, anything at all, she had learned that love was one bet she was not willing, to take—love only ended with heartbreak.

Of all of the people in the house, she and Chance were the last people who needed to further their relationship. Chance needed to concentrate on his newly acquired daughter. Starling needed him. She needed love. And she needed to find closure following her mother's untimely death. Any child who shut herself away from the world so dramatically needed help the most. Though Harper could try to connect with the girl, the one who held the lone key was Chance.

Chance admitted he knew nearly zero about how to deal with a teenage nymph. To be honest, Harper barely had a clue either. A teenage girl was an enigma—not quite woman, but no longer a child; able to love, but unable to love those closest to her. As different as Starling was, with her quiet demeanor and standoffish ways, beneath it all she was still a teen. She was still a child who had to be aching after the loss of the person dearest to her, yet she was forced to be a woman out of the circumstances of her past and present.

Of the numerous inspirational posters Harper had seen on her email and social media, one clicked into her mind—*the first step is always the hardest*. Maybe those cliché little posters were right. Maybe the first step with Starling would be the hardest, but it was a step that needed to be taken.

Harper pushed herself out of bed, and caught a glimpse of herself in the mirror. Her normally brilliant eyes carried the dullness created from a lack of sleep and too many worries. She walked to her suitcase and flipped it open. Her shirts and pants were divided, each item folded at an exact dimension to match the article of clothing beneath.

Her thoughts moved to Chance. Would he be able to handle the journey he was going to have to undertake with Starling? Could he handle the pressures and needs of the teenager? Would he even be able to take the first step—or would he and the girl keep each other at arm's length while the time passed until she was of an age to take care of herself?

Last night had proven he had the ability to open up and share, but sharing with a sullen teenager was far different than sharing with a woman who lay in his arms. Starling had no reason to feel anything for Chance, at least nothing approaching affection.

If anything, Chance had failed. He had failed to know Starling was alive. He'd never reached out to Carey, had never known he had a child, and now that Starling was alone the State wanted him to take control of her life? It was no wonder that the girl barely spoke or addressed them—and Harper couldn't blame her.

Harper slipped on a pair of finely pressed khaki pants and one of her least expensive cashmere sweaters. She feared going downstairs and facing the fallout of last night's mistake. It wouldn't surprise her, after her track record with relationships, if Chance had already slipped out with his teenage daughter in tow. So many times in her life she'd had a man leave her bed in the night never to set foot back into her life.

She could only hope Chance was different, that he wasn't the kind to bed her and leave. They had shared more than their bodies—they had shared something even more sacred—their secrets. He had shared a secret that most men in his position would have kept—he had put more trust in her than she could have ever expected from any man.

Picking up her brush, she pulled it through her long brown locks. What would Jenna think about all of this? This impromptu relationship raised more questions than Harper had ever thought possible.

Her sister had always been a free spirit, and as Harper thought of her, she imagined her sister sitting there watching her as she brushed her hair. It was a beautiful imagining and Harper hated to blink the vision away. Jenna seemed to nod and smile, giving her approval of Chance and the strange situation. Harper's eyes burned as they grew dry, forcing her to blink—making her picture of Jenna disappear.

Yes, Jenna would have given her permission. If she had spoken, Harper would have guessed her sister would have told her she was a fool for not wanting more—for not wanting to seize the chance to have a real relationship with the man.

Her mind drifted to Carey, the other nymph who had once taken a place in Chance's bed. Harper sucked in a surprised breath as she realized something she had missed. If Carey had gotten pregnant—something that most said was almost impossible for a nymph to do—then was it possible she would become pregnant as well?

Harper rushed from the room and hurried down the stairs. She needed to talk to Chance. Had he thought about what they had possibly done? Had he even come to realize there were not only emotional but possibly more dramatic consequences to their actions?

Harper tried to force her concern from showing on her face. She was probably getting upset over nothing—there was no way someone like her could become pregnant—not after they'd only had a one night affair.

Sitting at the '50s style metal-edged kitchen table was Starling. As usual, she was hunched over her notepad, making scrawling notes and strange drawings of intersecting circles and dashing lines. From across the room Harper could just make out the word "red" and what looked like some kind of bird.

The kitchen stood barren and lifeless behind the girl. The only items on the ugly mustard yellow countertops were a dust-covered toaster, a lonely coffeepot, and a butcher block filled with the mismatched handles of a variety of knives. The lonely room was just like the rest of the house, but something about the place was gradually changing—almost as if the place was coming alive with Harper and the girl's presence.

"Good morning, Starling," Harper said, trying to temper her residual fear. What if she was to become pregnant, as Carey had once done? Would she want a baby? How would this affect Starling? What would happen between her and Chance?

Chance was a good man, an honest man—except when he was playing cards—in which case the game was the focus of his life. He had made a point of telling her he would have to leave—that there were games he had to play. Poker was a profession that a man like Chance, the son of luck, would never be able to walk away from. It was the focus of his life and she had to doubt his focus would ever change.

His avoidance of a relationship in the shadows of the night had fallen on deaf ears, but now in the light of day her fears rose and were intensified with her new concerns. It hadn't mattered in the warmth of his arms, but now the entire situation made her feel like the lopsided picture she had seen at the lawyer's office—one simple thoughtless action would cause the whole picture to come crashing to the ground.

Seeing how he dealt with Starling's situation made her more nervous. Here he was, given a chance to have a real life, a real family with this young woman, and instead he was only going to find a way to fit her into his drifting life. Anyone who attempted to have this man in their life would have to face the same treatment. He would never change. He'd never settle down. And she had no intention of following any man.

Starling looked up from her book for a quick second. "Morning," she said in a voice barely above a whisper. Her skin was porcelain white and her hair was still wet from her bath.

Harper walked through the small dining room attached to the kitchen. "Are you hungry?"

Starling shook her head and looked back down at her paper.

"Are you sure?" Harper continued, hoping for more than a simple answer.

Starling didn't answer, and a new tear started in Harper's poorly stitched heart.

"Well, how about this?" Harper asked, even though she knew she was mostly talking to herself. "How about I run down to the store and get some groceries. When I come back I can cook you and your dad up some breakfast? Would you like that?"

Starling glanced up. "Chance left."

Harper's stomach lurched.

"What?"

"He. Left."

"Did he leave a note?"

The girl lifted her gaze and gave Harper a look that would have made the most hardened mother's skin prickle.

"I'll take that as a no."

Starling's eyebrow rose as if Harper was undeserving of a verbal answer. The tear in her heart widened.

He had slipped out. He had left her. And even more, he'd left her to care for this wearing teenager—and possibly the beginnings of another child. The softness she felt for the man melted away and was replaced by the harsh pangs of anger.

"Did he say where he was going?" Harper tried to sound calm and unaffected as she opened the fridge. She stared into the gleaming white abyss with only a few stray bottles of condiments and a box of baking soda as she waited for an answer that didn't come. She stared at the empty shelves and realized that the last thing she wanted was to eat. She shut the door and turned back to the teen. "Did he say anything?"

Starling shook her head, as if it made no difference to her whether or not Chance was there for her, or whether she would be in the care of Harper for an unknown amount of time. Did the girl have no feelings? Or had the wolves of her past forced her to hide her emotions, like they were some weakness that the predators could prey upon?

Most teenagers would have been dealing in some type of hysterics at this point, hating the world for the loss of their mother and hating life because of the injustice of their loss. But not Starling.

If Starling was the type who avoided the pain of the world, Harper didn't want to force the girl to face things she wasn't ready for. If anything, perhaps the best thing Harper could do was simply be there for the girl who pulsed with unspeakable loneliness. Starling had lost so much, and now the one person that they both—well, at least Harper—had trusted to take the girl in and protect her was gone as well.

The familiar sound of pen scratching on paper permeated through the kitchen as Harper made her way to the counter and grabbed the coffee pot from the machine.

"You a coffee drinker, Starling?"

"Yes."

"How do you take it?" She took the coffee pot and stuck it under the faucet and let it fill.

Almost out of habit, Harper brushed her hand over the counter, collecting the dust, which littered its surface. She rubbed her dust-covered hand down her leg, leaving behind traces of her sister's presence.

Starling shrugged.

"You're not a cream and sugar girl? I have to admit I'm a bit of a sucker for sweets. I guess it's my one weakness."

Starling's eyebrow arched. "Aren't you a nymph?"

"Does everyone in the whole world know my secret?"

The teen glanced up at the ceiling. "I have it from a good source."

Chance must have let it slip. "What about you? You a nymph like your mom or lucky like your dad?" She stepped up to the starting line of their relationship.

A light filled Starling's blue eyes. Harper hadn't noticed the girl's eyes before, the way the blue was about the same color of the ocean on the Washington coast. Starling blinked and the light flickered out, leaving only the cold blue waves and the girl's normal reserve. "I'm just a nymph."

This was the closest she and the girl had come to having a normal conversation and Harper didn't know if she wanted to risk the progress she had made in befriending the girl by asking another question. Yet the young woman had opened the door to an onslaught of questions that had wandered through Harper's mind for the last twenty-four hours and which seemed to grow only more burdensome.

Flipping off the faucet, Harper carried the coffee pot to the little white Mr. Coffee and filled the reservoir. Opening the cupboard, she pulled out the filters and an ancient red plastic bucket of coffee. Beside the bucket was a little plastic jar of powdered creamer and sugar packets, as if Jenna, who always drank black coffee, had known Harper would be there looking for her guilty pleasures. She peeked around the cupboard door as she pushed it closed, trying to catch one last glimpse of her sister's touch.

"So?" Harper asked, putting in the coffee filter and pouring a bit of coffee into the paper.

"Hmm?"

Harper clicked on the coffee maker and turned to face the teen. "Do you have a supernatural gift in addition to being a nymph?" The sputters and gurgles of the pot filled the quiet space between the two women and the rich scent of hot coffee started to fill the small kitchen.

"What do you care? You're going to leave."

The air rushed out of her. "I'm sorry about the loss of your mom, Starling. I truly am. It's not fair you have to go through this. You don't deserve to have lost your mom. Not now. Not ever."

Starling glanced down at the brown, cracked linoleum floor. She opened her mouth to speak, but paused for a moment. "It's not fair."

"As I've come to learn, nothing in life is fair. Sometimes those who deserve to die are made king and those that are most needed are the first to be struck down."

"I didn't need her." Starling's voice was scratchy from lack of use and she cleared her throat. "My mother needed me."

"That doesn't make what happened to your mom any easier—I know."

"You don't know."

Harper glanced around the dusty kitchen. "I know very well how much it hurts to lose the person you love the most."

The young woman raised her gaze and stopped just before their eyes met, almost as if she was looking at Harper's neck rather than her face. "At least your sister is happy."

"What?" Harper leaned back, letting the counter support her.

"Jenna. Is. Happy," Starling repeated.

"Starling, she can't be happy. Jenna is dead." Hadn't the girl heard the news of her sister's demise?

"I know."

Was the teenager trying to play some kind of sick game with her mind? Harper was already having a hard enough time trying to understand and come to terms with Chance's revelation and its possible consequences—was the girl trying to make her think she was losing her track on reality?

Harper turned back to the coffee pot and watched the brown liquid drip into the steadily filling pot. "Sweetheart, I know you've been through a lot, but teasing me isn't going to make anything better."

"I don't tease." Starling turned to the table and lifted up her notebook. "Your sister is here. She woke me."

There were a lot of things Harper had seen in her long life, but seeing ghosts was a little too far out of her comfort zone. She was a scientist, a woman who dealt with clear actions and reactions. She wasn't the type who would believe in ghosts.

Then again, there was something about the girl, maybe her no-nonsense and quiet ways, which seemed to make such a thing almost possible. The girl was so different that her revelation almost seemed to fit her—the dark-haired and dark-spirited nymph.

"Okay. If that's true, how did you talk to her?" Harper tried to keep her disbelief from causing a strange inflection in her words. If the girl could do what she said she could, Harper needed to support her. As strange as talking to the dead was, it couldn't be said her own shape-shifting abilities would have been any less far-fetched to someone who hadn't known nymphs existed. In this case, an open mind was her only option.

Starling turned back to her salt and pepper composition book. She opened up the pages and lifted her pen. "Watch."

The nib of the pen moved in tight circles even before she let the ink release upon the paper. As she moved the pen down, the circles slowed, but her movements made deep black circular gouges. The shapes changed as she moved the pen around and around, and soon they became deep cutting gashes.

"Ask for a spirit to make contact," Starling said.

Harper didn't know what to ask, but there was only one spirit with whom she wished to speak. A lump started in her throat and goose bumps rose on her skin. "Are there any spirits who'd like to make contact? Jenna?" Her voice wavered.

"She's here … " Starling's face went blank and her eyes closed. Her left hand dropped down to the open book, but the pen in her right hand kept moving in rhythmic motions. The pen jerked. The nib dug deep, scratching against the paper so hard that it was a wonder the paper didn't rip. "R" formed on the paper. It was followed by an "E." The pen moved and its ink merged into a "D" on the paper, making the word "red."

"Jenna, what do you mean by *red*?" Harper looked up, searching for some kind of answer.

The front door of the house opened, letting in a puff of cold winter air and making the goose bumps upon Harper's arms raise higher.

"Hello? You ladies awake?" Chance called, slamming the door shut behind him.

Starling's writing stopped. The white plastic pen fell from her fingers and clattered on the table.

"Uh, yeah." Harper looked around hoping she could catch a glimpse of her ghostly sister, but she saw nothing out of the normal. "We're in here."

Chance walked into the kitchen his arms full of groceries. A red plastic bread bag peaked out from over the top of one of the bags.

For a moment, Harper was angry for his leaving without telling her where he was going or when he'd be back, but her anger was replaced with a sense of relief. "Where have you been?"

He dropped the bags down onto the counter and began unloading their contents.

"I didn't want another popcorn shrimp incident." He pushed a carton of milk into the fridge and shut the door. "What's going on?"

Harper stared down at the mysterious symbols and words in Starling notebook. "Starling, do you want to tell him, or should I?"

Chapter Twelve

The last bits of the scrambled eggs wiggled around Chance's plate as if they were as uncomfortable with the conversation as he was. Harper sat her fork down on the edge of her plate with a clink.

"What do you think?"

"I'm thinking a lot of things." He tried to give Harper a look that would remind her of how he hadn't wanted to force Starling into spilling her secrets.

"Thank you, Starling, for telling me about Jenna. I know it must have been hard for you," Harper said, her voice soft and caring.

"Yeah, thanks," Chance echoed, but his heart wasn't in it. He had expected many things from his daughter, anger, resentment, and even the revelation that she was a nymph, but he hadn't expected this. He wasn't prepared to hear that his daughter could speak to the dead. He was at a loss.

"Yeah," Starling replied with a shrug.

"Let me get this right. So you can speak to the dead through writing?" Chance tried not to stare at Starling's composition book, which sat as the centerpiece of the table.

"Yeah." Starling ripped a corner from the piece of toast on her plate and popped it into her mouth. It was nice to see his daughter eating. It was the most normal thing he had seen her do since she'd arrived into their lives. It was too bad the little sense of normalcy was so fleeting.

He'd never met anyone who could actually talk to the dead. He'd seen a few late night infomercials in which the psychics claimed they could connect with the dead, but until this moment he'd thought it was all bullshit. Yet, sitting here and staring at the black-haired young woman he couldn't deny she had a gift. He'd seen it firsthand, the way the pen seemed to skim over the paper, making words given to Starling by a dead woman.

He glanced over at the word *Red*. Beneath Harper's sister's name was a series of lines and then the word *Find her. Help all.* Chills ran down his spine as he thought of all of the possible meanings for those simple words and what Jenna had meant by *red*—had she meant Carey's red hair, or something more sinister?

"Did your mother know about your abilities?"

Starling nodded again. "She could do it too."

Another of Carey's secrets he was only learning now—long after it would be of any help. "Have you been talking to her through your writing?"

Starling nodded.

"Can you hear the dead or do they just use you to write?" He stared at the black spiraled *M* at the end of *Find them.*

"Sometimes they talk."

Chance tore his gaze from the letter and tried to focus on the familiar eyes of a daughter he was only coming to know. "Does Carey talk to you?"

"I only listen."

If Starling was telling the truth and talking to her mother, then she could find out what really happened. The girl was only a day out from finding out about her mother's death; she couldn't be ready to talk about it. Or could she?

"Have you asked Carey how she died?"

Starling's chin moved down and she sent him a look from under her brows, which would have made lesser men question themselves, but he had every right to ask about her mother's death.

"Did she tell you if someone killed her?" he tried again.

"No." Starling's monosyllabic answer overflowed with contempt.

Why did talking to her have to be like pulling teeth? Was it her age? Or was she simply her mother's daughter? "Did you ask?"

"No."

Harper sat forward, almost as if she wanted to put a stop to his interrogation, but he shot her a look. "Why not?"

"Why would I?"

Harper shook her head, motioning for him to stop.

"Starling, don't you want to know what really happened to your mom?"

Starling shrugged.

"Could you at least try and find out?"

"Stop, Chance." Harper dropped her hands to the table as she stared at Starling. There were tears sliding down the girl's face.

"I'm … I'm sorry, Starling." The hope for answers which had only seconds ago been inflating suddenly seeped from him like a balloon let loose from a child's fingers. "I didn't mean to upset you."

"No. You meant to use me." Starling dropped her face in an effort to hide her tears. "Just like everyone else." Starling jumped up from her chair, upsetting it and letting it crash to the ground as she ran to Harper's guest room.

"Why did you do that?" Harper asked him as if she was accusing him of some evil misdeed.

"All I wanted to know was who was behind her mother's death. I swear I didn't mean to upset her."

Harper stood and picked up her and Starling's plates and walked them to the kitchen sink. "For someone who is supposed to know how to read people, you can be terrible at it."

"That's not true." Even as he spoke the words, he knew Harper was right. He'd pressed Starling too far. She was young and in pain. Chance stood up and walked his plate into the kitchen. He stopped beside Harper.

Harper sighed as she sat the plates down into the sink. "Chance, when you're playing poker, what do you do when you have a drawing hand? Do you show them your cards?"

"No." He sat his plate down on top of the others in the sink.

"What do you do?" Harper turned to face him.

"I don't know, depends on the opponents and the pot odds."

"What are pot odds?"

"In poker, if your odds of getting the card you need are higher than the odds of your bet in relation to the winning pot you go in. If not, you call."

"So, in other words, if you think you can win, you keep betting?"

He nodded. "Usually, if the pot odds are in my favor."

"What happens when you think you can't win? Do you make a bad bet or do you let it go and hope you'll get a better hand the next deal?"

It was a no-brainer; no one wanted to bleed chips. "You can chase the hand by calling or you can fold and wait to get back in the game and then make the smarter bet."

"What you just did with Starling was a bad bet, my friend. Now you are going to have to fight to get back in the game."

She pushed off from the sink and walked out of the kitchen without another word.

Chance felt like an ass. Harper was right—he had taken a low road to get Starling to talk, and hadn't been thinking about her and her feelings. He wasn't used to having to take women into consideration. Kodie was nothing like this—he was always just there, ready to brush up some players for the next game. He didn't get upset when Chance fucked up. Hell, Kodie had to half expect him to say something stupid—it just came with the territory. He was going to have to pick up his game with the women in his life—or else get the hell out.

But was running away the answer? If his past had taught him one thing, it was that running was a hell of a lot easier than facing things. Running away always let him get another perspective and, at least for a short time, forget.

He walked out of the kitchen and made his way upstairs, hoping the entire way he wouldn't run into Harper or Starling. He needed a moment to think, to come up with the pot odds. Were the odds better to stay or was it smarter to walk away?

Chance pushed open the door to his guest room and grabbed a handful of clean clothes and his shower gear. He grabbed his tired white towel that had turned slightly yellow from the ravages of age and the thousands of nights he had spent in cheap hotels. It struck him how he was a bit like this old worn-out towel—there was always some soiled spot to remind him of his actions from the past.

Throwing the towel and his clothes on the bathroom counter, he turned to the shower. He couldn't remember the last time he'd taken a shower in a place that wasn't in a hotel. He hadn't lived in a real house in a long time. The best he had was a mini storage unit half filled with castoffs from the life he'd shared with Carey. After the divorce, he'd hit the road and hadn't looked back, but here he was, faced with all of his mistakes.

Dropping to his knees he laid his face on the cold porcelain of the tub. The cold felt good against his skin. Unlike the revelation his daughter had made, it was something real—something tangible. He reached up and pulled the old-fashioned shower knob. The pipes moaned and a deep thumping echoed up from the bowels of the house. He pushed the knob back down. Maybe this was the one thing he could fix.

He stood up and walked out of the bathroom, then out of the house to his truck. In the bed was a red aluminum box of tools. He turned around to head back into the house, but was met by Harper standing in the front door, her hand on her hip.

"Where do you think you're going? Do you really think you could run away?" She sounded like an enraged mother, ready to take him out at the knees over her unfounded fear—well, not that her fears were not without some merit, but he wouldn't have left—not like this, not without so much as a word to the only women in his life.

"Just because I left Carey doesn't mean that I'm going to run away from Starling. Or you."

"You say you're not running away. But you are going to Vegas." She could barely look at him. "You are running. You're running away from me."

"Harper … " He stopped beside her and sat down his tools. "I thought we understood that this couldn't be anything." No matter how much he was attracted to her. No matter how badly he wanted to pull her into his arms or taste her flavor on his lips.

"It's fine. I get it," Harper said with an edge of anger to her voice.

"Don't be angry with me. Please." He reached out and put his hands on her arms, but she pulled away.

"What are you doing with your toolbox?" Harper asked as she avoided the uncomfortable silence that had settled between them.

"The shower isn't working. I was just getting going to try my hand at fixing the thing."

"I was going to call a plumber. You don't need to worry about it."

"I'm staying here with Starling. It's the least I can do to help." Besides, if he wasn't working, or keeping busy, he would be forced to repel the tension in the house. Around every corner he would feel Starling's growing dislike and Harper's fear that he would disappear.

"When are you thinking you and Starling are going to leave?"

He wanted to touch and comfort her, but after being rebuffed he forced his hands to rest at his sides. "I'm planning on heading out in the morning. The game in Vegas is starting the day after tomorrow and Kodie and I have to be there early—we have to get a feel for the other players."

"You taking Starling with you?"

"I think so. I guess there really isn't any alternative."

"You know, you could get a house here in Worley. You could settle down and let her finish school. She's a senior—she only has a few months left. If you wanted, you could rent an apartment—maybe even this house—and have a normal life."

Something about the idea struck him as beautiful. There he could be with Starling at his side, living together as a family until Starling could finish her last bit of high school.

On the other side of the argument, in order to follow that dream, he would have to give up his life, his hopes of striking it rich, and living a life most bachelors could only dream about. He'd been living the good life up until Kodie took the money from Nate. And with that debt looming, now wasn't the time for Chance to run off and start playing house. He'd told his friend he would help him out; he'd told Kodie he'd win the tournament. If he didn't he hated to think what Nate would do to his best friend.

And about Starling … Well, the only thing that kept Starling tied to this place, except Harper—who herself was moving— was Starling's high school. Starling could finish her education anywhere. Hell, she could even get her diploma from one of those online schools. Maybe. Other than her school, this placed was only filled with the horrific memories of her mother, the dead, and what had to be the terrors of her past—all the poor girl did was live with ghosts.

Maybe Harper was the one who had it all wrong. Maybe a little travel and life experience was exactly what Starling needed. She could step out of the confines of her own mind for a while. Maybe he could even find others like her—others who connected with spirits. There was one thing he knew for sure—they wouldn't find anyone else like Starling, no one with a gift, in the little dot on the map that was Worley, Idaho.

Even though they were so close he could feel the heat of her body radiating from her, she was a world away. She didn't understand all he had to lose, all he owed. She may have thought she knew him, but she didn't have a clue. "I know what you're trying to say, Harper, and I appreciate it. But I have to do what I have to do."

"There's no way you would ever be willing to stop drifting, is there?"

His mind slipped back to thoughts of Carey and the time they'd spent together in this town. He'd always been looking for the next big thing, always trying to make ends meet when there was never enough—not enough time, money, not even love. He couldn't bear the thought of going through the motions of that type of life again.

"You, a nymph, are going to judge me for something you don't understand? You of all people should know that sometimes we have to do things other people don't understand in order to survive. I carry my own curse."

She stepped back in affront. "How dare you use what I told you against me? You are lucky. You aren't cursed. You can't possibly understand what it's like to be a nymph—always carrying the weight of knowing you can't have love—that you can't make another person truly happy—knowing you always have to walk away from the one thing you want more than anything else."

"You think I don't want a home? A real life?"

"That's not what I said."

"Look," he said, "I want love. I want a real life. I get tired of traveling around, winning and losing, but never really getting anywhere. But I don't have anything to offer anyone. I don't have anything in my life except poker—and now a daughter who I'm going to have to figure out how to raise. You deserve a man better than me. You deserve a man who can give you everything you want, a man who can make you happy."

She looked up at him and there were tears in her sparkling eyes. Behind the tears, her amber eyes were filled with hundreds of years of pain—all which seemed to be captured in her heart and trying in vain to escape through her gaze. He couldn't stop himself from wrapping his arms around her and pulling her into his chest. "I'm only trying to protect you, just like you are trying to protect Starling and me." Her body tensed in his arms, but after a moment she relaxed—as if she knew there was no point in fighting.

He took in her soft scent as he leaned down and kissed the top of her head.

His phone chirped from his back pocket.

Harper wiggled from his arms and wiped her hands under her eyes, hiding any tears that had slipped out of her control.

Chance dropped his empty arms. Numbly, he reached back and extracted the phone from his pocket. A text message popped up from Kodie. "You ready to go, man? Vegas waits."

Chapter Thirteen

The red box of tools sat inside the front door of the house, reminding Harper of Chance's leaving. He'd made some lame excuse about how Kodie had needed him. She had seen through his feeble attempt to get away from the house—she tried to tell herself she didn't care.

He'd only left to pick up Kodie, but she couldn't harness the uncontrollable fear that he may never return. She could only hope he would come back again so she could at least tell him one last good bye before they forever parted ways.

Harper grabbed an empty cardboard box and pushed it open. It was time. It was time to start emptying the house, to move on, and come to terms with her sister's death. Everything needed to get back to normal. She was sick of this constant emotional rollercoaster. Chance had made it clear that there was nothing left here for him—and there was certainly nothing left here for her. The comfort of her job waited for her and she couldn't wait to get home to the warm blanket of her routine.

The romance novels filled the box to the brim. Harper stood up and walked to the table beside the door where she had sat the lawyer's paperwork and opened one of the drawers. She couldn't help but stare at Jenna's keys. The mismatched keys had shifted slightly, disturbing the dust on the table around them. There were so many things, so many keys, to Jenna's life—she would never get to know what most of them meant, or who Jenna had become in the last few years. Harper had missed so much.

In the drawer sat an old Sharpie and a mass of accumulated pens in a variety of cheap plastic and covered in the logos of several businesses. The pen on the top read *Shaw Pharmaceuticals*. Harper reached down and picked up the pen and the marker.

One of her friends from college had gone on to work at Shaw Pharmaceuticals, but aside from the company being a rival of Merckson, she knew little about them except they were located in Las Vegas. She dropped the pen back in the drawer and slid it shut carefully in an effort to leave her sister's keys undisturbed.

Uncapping the marker, she wrote *Giveaway* across the top of the book filled box. It made her heart ache to think about having to do this in every room of the house. Each box would be another piece of Jenna slipping away and another slice into Harper's heart. She would never be able to understand why the men at the God forsaken Diamond Bar Ranch had done what they had to Jenna.

Ariadne Papadakis, the new leader of the Sisterhood of Epione, had told her the men had wanted to create a hybrid species of horse to use in the rodeo circuit. Jenna had been taking a fertility drug, Clomiphene, in an attempt to get pregnant up until her captors had found out the truth of her being a swan-shifter. Even if Jenna had wanted a baby it seemed a long stretch for her to become involved with the murderers—in fact, it had cost her life.

The floor creaked behind her drawing her attention.

"Harper?" Starling stood at the end of the hallway looking at her. She had her hair pulled back and a black backpack slung over her shoulder. "Can you take me to school?"

Never in her wildest dreams had Harper thought the young woman would have wanted to go to school—not after everything that had happened.

"Are you sure you want to go?"

Starling nodded and dropped her gaze to the ground.

If Starling was anything like Harper, she probably wanted to find something normal in all of the rapid changes in her life. She probably wanted to hold on to the one thing that remained a constant and served as a challenge, which required her mind to move away from the events happening in her private life.

"Okay," Harper said, standing up. "You'll have to show me where to go. I'm afraid I've never dropped anyone off at high school before."

It was hard to tell by looking at Starling's downcast face, but for a moment she could have sworn she saw a flicker of a smile.

Chapter Fourteen

The boxes were beginning to stack up in the living room, making it look more like a mini-storage and less like a home. The clock ticked away, marking each second of Harper's loneliness. Though she'd lived the last twenty years alone, she'd not been this lonely since she and Jenna had parted ways.

She gazed up at the clock and watched the damned second hand tick by as if it was the clock that controlled the arrival of Chance and Starling back into her life.

What was she going to do when they left? No amount of watching the clock was going to bring back the sounds of Starling's scribbling and Chance's footfalls down the hall—nothing was going to bring back the sounds of living. No. Instead she would fall back into her old life and her old routines, but she'd never again get the chance to pretend to be a part of a family.

Every moment that ticked by, every second wasted, was a chance lost, a memory not made, and a change that would never come.

Guilt gnawed at her like a hungry pup as she started to take down Jenna's knickknacks and pack them into a box. She shouldn't have been so needy. They had talked about how they couldn't have a relationship—he was only keeping true to his word. And he had every right.

He needed to learn how to incorporate Starling into his life and to do this he couldn't focus on having a relationship. Her mind turned to how he had handled Starling's automatic writing. He'd seemed like he'd been lost in a sea of confusion. And she'd been so hard on him. She had no right to criticize him for doing things differently than she would have liked. He was a grown man.

She had criticized Chance for screwing up his second chance at life, but she was no better. She'd found a great job, a great home, but she'd failed on so many other levels. She had been completely alone. She'd poured herself into her work and lost everything that really mattered. At least Chance was living the life he wanted to live. She couldn't say the same for herself.

And here she was, given another chance at having more than strangers in her life, and she was repeating her old mistakes, once again trying to hold onto something she couldn't have at the same time trying to push him away. With everything she did: love, life, family—everything except her work—she failed.

The marker's bitter licorice smell wafted up to her as she wrote *Giveaway* across the top of a box filled with the little porcelain figurines with soft pastel colors finely brushed over their cherubic cheeks. She could barely stand to look at them anymore, the way they smiled while the world collapsed around them. Their big eyes seemed to follow her around, mocking her with their ever-present glee.

Harper stood up and stepped back, her foot brushing against Chance's red box of tools. The need to escape the torrent of her thoughts followed her just like the little porcelain dolls' gaze—the need grated at her, but unlike the dolls she couldn't simply pack her feelings away.

She dropped her hands down to her lower belly and the simple action made her think about the possibility of a pregnancy. Just that morning it had seemed like such a revolting possibility. Yet the more she thought about it, the more the idea of a baby tucked safely inside of her belly seemed like a precious gift. Nymphs had had babies, but it was so rare that Harper had never met anyone except Carey who'd borne a child. And though she knew the required physical action necessary to make a human baby, it wasn't the same for nymphs. No—for nymphs there were many myths surrounding conception, and sprinkled in there was always a certain amount of magic.

Once during one of her trips to Croatia, she had heard a myth. An old nymph had talked about a nymph named Cetina, a dolphin-shifter, who was among the first of her kind. One day many thousands of years ago, before the time of Epione, Cetina had been crying at the bottom of a hill when Zeus came down from the heavens and sat beside her. Zeus asked her why she was crying and Cetina told him she had always wanted a baby. Zeus, being the sexual beast he was, tried to convince her that if she made love to him in the moonlight as they bathed in the salt of her tears, she would conceive a child.

Cetina was no fool and knew of Zeus and his sexual appetite and his narcissistic need to fornicate with every woman with whom he crossed paths. "Zeus," Cetina said, "if you promise me our union will result in a child, I'll be forever grateful, but if you leave me barren, for the rest of time no other nymphs will lay with you."

Zeus eagerly agreed and made love to the beautiful young nymph and left. After many weeks of waiting, nothing happened and Cetina knew that she had fallen victim to the empty promises of the sexually ravenous god. Again she wept and wept until her tears became a river and Cetina, drying up, turned to stone.

The Neolithic people named the river Cetina in honor of the woman who had been tricked by the gods, and it was said those who wished to become pregnant, nymph or human, merely had to bathe in the demigoddess's tears after a night of making love and a baby of good fortune would come. Around 1912, huge hydroelectric power plants were built on the river, disturbing its flow and the magic the river contained. Since then, no nymph had been able to get pregnant.

Somehow Carey had found a way around the magic of the river in order to get pregnant. Had she gotten pregnant on purpose? Or had the pregnancy been some trick of the fates?

Harper's fingers trembled over her stomach as she caught a glimpse of a future that she had never before thought possible—strollers, bottles, night feedings, and lullabies. For a second she envisioned Chance standing by her side, a baby cradled in his arms.

A pained laugh escaped her lips before she could hold it back. Chance would never stay in one place long enough to share a family with her. There was no future for them—no matter how much she dreamed.

She picked up Chance's toolbox. She couldn't depend on him for anything. No. Not even to fix a damn faucet.

Her footfalls thundered through the empty house as she made her way to the upstairs bathroom. She dropped the cold metal box onto the floor. She didn't have a clue how to start. Harper took out a screwdriver. Locating the faucet's screws she fumbled them loose and pulled the handle from the wall. Then she unscrewed the faceplate.

The door to the bathroom flew open, making her jump. The screwdriver dropped from her hand and clattered in the porcelain tub.

"Oh look!" Kodie exclaimed. "Ms. Trips-a-Lot is a plumber too." His laughter filled the tiled bathroom.

"She's always a surprise." Chance stepped beside Kodie in the doorway. "Where's Starling?"

"She wanted to go to school, so I dropped her off. I thought she should have one last chance to say goodbye to her friends before you took her traipsing off for some poker game."

Chance nodded, but didn't seem thrown by her jab. "Did you remember to turn off the main water line?"

Her cheeks burned. Another five minutes and they would have found her standing in a pool. "I wouldn't be doing this at all if you had just finished what you started."

He looked at her as if he understood she was talking about more than simply fixing the faucet. "I'm sorry, but I'm back."

"For how long?"

Chance got a twisted, guilty look on his face. "Kodie and I have to leave tonight. We don't have a choice."

"There's always a choice." Her anger at his leaving couldn't be contained. He had to know that his decisions affected not only him, but Starling—and her.

"No. In this case I have to go to the games. I made a promise I have to keep."

"Lots of promises, aren't there?" She stood up and wiped off her knees a little too hard.

"Stumbelina," Kodie said in a light-hearted tone, "why don't you come with us?"

"Kodie, no … " Chance started. He caught her eyes and stopped.

"I can't." She couldn't tear her gaze away from Chance's confused face.

"Why can't you?" Kodie shrugged. "Ain't no reason for you to be sticking around here. From the state of this bathroom you ain't much of a plumber."

"I have to get the house on the market and get back to Seattle. My job is waiting."

"How much time do you have off? Our little trip to Vegas will only take a couple of days. In and out. Real quick."

Chance gripped the doorframe as if he was about to rip it from the wall. Something about his anxiety made Harper consider Kodie's offer. She and Chance couldn't have a relationship, but maybe they could at least build a friendship. Starling would need her.

There would be little chance of her convincing Chance to settle down for Starling, but maybe she could make him see how important it was that Starling lead a normal life during her last year of high school.

And more than anything … if she went with them, there wouldn't be another goodbye. At least not for a few days. She could go on pretending she wasn't alone in the world.

"I don't think it's a good idea, Harper. I mean, I want you there and everything—"

"Great," she said, cutting Chance off. "Then it's settled, I'll be going to Vegas with you. You all need someone to take care of Starling for a few days while you're playing in your tournament. She can't be running around Vegas on her own."

"This isn't a great idea, Harper. I don't want you to get hurt."

She was already hurt. All she could do now was learn to deal with the pain.

Harper leaned back against the wall, letting it support her. Behind her something fell into the tub with a loud thump. She turned. Sitting next to her discarded screwdriver was a package. Brown tape circled a familiar plastic square, just like before—this time the only thing missing was the shrimp box.

Harper picked up the package of drugs. On its surface was a logo with the letters "S" and "P." She'd seen the logo before—on the pen in the table drawer by the front door. The logo belonged to Shaw Pharmaceuticals.

"What in the hell is that?" Kodie asked.

"It's more evidence that I need to get out of here and get to Las Vegas."

Chapter Fifteen

The white powder was much the same as the package they had pulled out of the freezer—with one exception. There was a small stamp on the bag that read "*S P*." Chance turned the bag of drugs over in his hands. "Are you sure that this isn't heroin?"

Harper shrugged. "Without a chemical analysis it is hard to say, but assuming this packet actually came from Shaw Pharmaceuticals, it's hard to imagine that it's heroin—or any other illicit drug."

Something about this struck him as odd. "What do you know about Shaw Pharmaceuticals?"

Harper's face scrunched the way it always did when she was thinking. "It's just a normal pharmaceutical company. Right now they're working on a synthetic form of a drug used in the treatment of breast cancer."

"Is there some reason your sister would be in possession of a large amount of one of their drugs? Was she sick? Nymphs can't get breast cancer, can they?"

"A nymph? What are you talking about, *Chance*?" Harper jerked and looked over at Kodie, as if reminding him to stay silent about her secret.

"I'm sorry … " Chance stammered. He hadn't meant to out her. Never. He hadn't been thinking. "I didn't mean … "

Kodie gave Harper his most heartwarming smile. "Don't worry about it, Stumbelina—your secret's safe with me."

Harper glared at Chance. "You had no right to tell anyone my secret. I thought I could trust you, but once again, I was wrong." She turned around and walked out of the room, leaving him with the guilt that always seemed to swallow him in her wake.

He handed Kodie the parcel of drugs and chased after her. He'd made a mistake, yes. But Kodie was the person he'd trusted more than any other for the last decade—he'd never had to keep anything, aside from his cards, a secret from him. She had to be made to understand she could trust the man with the same confidence.

"Harper, stop," Chance called out after her as he moved down the hallway toward the stairs.

She spun around, her hair flipping around her like the blades of a fan. "How dare you … " she seethed.

"I'm sorry. It's not like he wouldn't have found out anyway, now you're going to go to Vegas with us. He knows about Carey and nymphs—he would have figured it out as soon as the men started to flock."

"That's not the point, and you know it." She drew her arms in tight over her chest. Even though she was angry he couldn't help but notice the way her breasts pressed hard against the purple fabric of her shirt, almost as if they were as angry with him as she was.

"Why do you always have to find some reason to push me away? To be angry with me? In case you haven't noticed, it's not as if I want to be on the move with a teenage girl."

"If you don't want to go, then why are you running off like there's fire under your feet? You just can't seem to get away from me fast enough, can you?"

"This has nothing to do with you, Harper."

"That's a lie and you know it." Harper glared at him. "The truth is that you can't stand getting close to another person. The only person you think you can trust is him … " She gestured at Kodie in the bathroom. "If you didn't run all the time, you'd figure out there are more people in this world you can trust … if you just let yourself be open."

"I *was* open with you, Harper. I told you who and what I really am—how is that not enough for you?" His sudden anger seemed to catch her off-guard as if she had assumed he wouldn't fight back, that he was just another person she could control.

"You told me the truth about how you came to be, but don't think your confession told me anything. Yes, your father was a god, but that doesn't tell me who you are."

"What is it you want to know?"

Harper dropped her arms. "I want to really know *you*. Not this bullshit version of yourself you fed me the other night. You can't stand there and pretend you're perfect—that you're not hiding something."

"What makes you think I'm hiding something?" Chance jerked before he could stop himself.

"You can't tell me you don't feel something for me."

She was right. He did feel something for her. He did want more, but he couldn't give her what she needed. And because he cared for her, he couldn't keep her hoping that they could become something more. "I do have feelings for you, Harper. But I have lied."

Harper leaned back against the wall as she seemed to collect herself. "If you even want to be my friend, you're going to need to tell me the truth."

"Fine." Chance stuffed his hand in his back pocket. "You want to know the truth about me and what a terrible man I have been?"

Harper nodded.

"I knew about the curse of the nymphs. I knew about what and who Carey was and I left her because I was scared. I was scared about getting involved with someone who wouldn't want to love me back. Hell, I was scared about falling in love with someone who *would* love me back. Plain and simple, I wasn't ready for anything real."

"Are you ready now?"

"If you want the honest truth ... I don't really know. But I do know there are some things which have to be handled before I can think about taking that step with anyone ... no matter how badly I want to."

A smile flickered on Harper's lips, but was replaced with a look of concern. "And those things are?"

"As you know, Kodie there," Chance said, jabbing his thumb in the direction of the bathroom, "decided it was a good idea to take a loan from a loan shark."

"I still can't believe it, what kind of a moron—"

"Hey, you two ... don't forget I can hear you," Kodie called from the bathroom.

Chance snorted. "It's funny how well you can hear when you're supposed to be minding your own business."

"Hey now," Kodie answered, a playful edge to his voice. "You know there isn't anything better than two lovers squabbling."

Chance stepped next to Harper and slid his arms around her shoulders. "Let's go downstairs where we can finish talking in *private*." He looked back over his shoulder at the bathroom door. "And Kodie, while you are in there, why don't you make yourself useful and put the faucet back together?"

"Got it, boss."

"I know I'm being a pain in the ass," Harper said, "but you're not getting out of this that easily. I know there's more you're hiding."

"You are right in one thing ... you are a pain in the ass."

She pulled out of his arms and sauntered down the steps. "I'm not the bigger pain between the two of us—not by a long shot."

"Hey, it's not like you have been the picture of honesty either." He followed her down the steps, out the back door and onto the small wooden deck. The rickety deck overlooked a hillside where one winter-chilled tree stood naked, exposed and vulnerable to the harsh slaps of the icy air.

"I don't know what the hell you are talking about. I've never told anyone else about what I am, but I told you, didn't I? And you let my secret slip. Why would I trust you again?"

"I'm sorry. I should have never let it slip. But that doesn't change that you're hiding things from me as well."

"Like what?" she scoffed, making him wonder if he had gotten her all wrong. For a second, he considered shutting his mouth and stopping right there. Yet there was no point in him giving her everything he had if she wasn't going to give back in return. He needed to know she was a bet he could take, or if he should walk away.

"What happened between you and your sister? You seem to have loved her so much, I can't figure it out—why all of a sudden you'd pack up your things and start a new life. You don't seem like the type to run."

"I ... you're right ... " Harper tried to find her words. "I'm not the type to run. But I'm also not the type to sit around and watch someone take my life and ruin their own."

"What are you talking about?"

"My sister and I used to love to shift into swans and make our own little bevy. We'd take to the sky almost every day. It was fabulous. We would use our shift to get over whatever was bothering us, but one day she didn't want to go and then the next and the next."

Harper stepped to the edge of the deck and leaned over the railing, dangerously close to falling over the weak boards that supported her. Instinctively, Chance stepped toward her, ready to catch her if she fell. "Why?"

"At the time I was married. He seemed like a great man. Smart, motivated, and, as it turned out, terribly narcissistic. He wasn't happy with me—I was the one who always stayed close to the ground, the one who never took a chance and only took pleasure from things that were static … What can I say, other than I just wasn't enough for him."

"But your sister was?"

"They didn't get together right away. Jenna tried to stop from having feelings, but he needed to possess her. What man doesn't have some fantasy about sisters?" She hid her face, but Chance could tell she was crying from the soft trembling of her shoulders. "It wasn't long after he fell in love with Jenna before he was taken by the curse, making it more than clear that he'd never loved me. I lost everything. My husband. My sister. My life. I never want to be in that place … that personal hell brought on by love … ever again."

He stepped behind her and pushed her hair away from her neck, exposing the little black tattoo at its base. He moved closer, basking in the floral scent of her shampoo which almost overpowered her subtle scents of fresh air mixed with a hint of down. "Any man who wouldn't be happy with a wonderful woman like you would be a fool. You're so amazing. You're smart, and ambitious—you can't stop loving because of your past. You told me I need to be open … but maybe the one who really needs to be open is you. You need to be open to love. You need to live."

"Chance, I can't fall in love. I can't love a man knowing that he could die if I let my emotions go unchecked. And you know it. You always have."

She was right, he was afraid of loving—and of dying for love.

She moved to turn, but he dropped his hands to her hips and stopped her. His lips grazed the naked flesh at the base of her neck. She gasped as he touched her warm flesh.

"I know how much you like to be in control, but not this time." His voice took on the edge of command, rough and tender at the same time. She seemed to melt under his hands as he pushed his body against hers, letting her feel exactly what she did to him. If she ever doubted how badly he wanted her, she no longer could.

He trailed his kisses up the back of her neck and her body shuddered under his hands. He wished she had been wearing a skirt, something he could easily flip up so he could make love to her here and now, but she was sentenced to the confines of her perfect fitting jeans. Her downy soft hairs brushed against his face, further charging his need to possess her body. How could she do this to him every time they were close? Was it her nymph charms or was it something more? Was it possible that what he was feeling was more than lust? More than the primal need to feel her beneath him?

His fingers twisted underneath her shirt and he found her soft, warm skin. Harper pushed against him and rubbed her body up and down his length, making him moan into the curls of her hair. She sucked in a breath as she rubbed again, faster, hungrier. He reached his fingers higher, pushing them under the wire bottom of her bra. He found her hard beneath his touch. The cloth of her bra and shirt forced his fingers down, but he tried to be gentle as he ran her nipple between his fingers.

"Do you want me to go to Vegas with you?" Harper asked breathlessly.

"Mm hmm." He couldn't concentrate; her words seemed to be swimming through a cloud of swirling lust.

There was a knock on the glass sliding door behind them and Harper slipped from Chance's arms. The door slid open. "Sorry, you two, but there's a phone call," Kodie interrupted. "The man says he's the principal of Starling's school. Apparently Starling is behind some kind of incident. You may want to take this."

Chapter Sixteen

She'd never been a parent, but Harper knew that whenever a principal called to report an "incident" there would be no good news to follow. There would be no awards to pick up, no sweet smiles, or slaps on the back. For the first time since they'd found out about Chance having a daughter, she wasn't envious. She shuddered to imagine sitting in the office, staring at the principal's austere white walls, filled with the nervous energy of someone who waited to be judged.

Chance turned the truck down the road that led to the high school. A tight scowl was planted on his face.

"I'm glad Kodie wanted to stay behind. I didn't need him cracking Little Miss Trips-A-Lot jokes," Harper said, trying to lighten the mood, or at the very least make the look of anger disappear from Chance's beautiful steely eyes.

Chance grumbled an unintelligible response, but the look on his face didn't flicker.

The knot in her stomach clenched tighter as she thought of how Starling had to be handling the pressure. Starling had already been through so much, it seemed unfair there were more battles to be fought. Yet in life, it always seemed when the disastrous ball of fate started rolling downhill, it only stopped once it had slammed into everything and everyone in its path.

If Starling was a normal girl, instead of a nymph, Harper knew the young woman would have been a mess as she waited for them in the principal's office. However, having watched how she handled the loss of her mother and her former life, Harper couldn't help but feel that Chance was probably taking the incident harder than his daughter. Starling had a way of being dismissive of the emotional turmoil surrounding her, but not Chance.

Harper passed a glance over at him, but nothing had changed—his eyes still carried the angry edge of a parent getting ready for a fight that centered on their child. It was hard to imagine him looking fiercer.

Chance pulled the truck to a stop as he parked in front of the beige high school building. The students' parking lot, which had been unoccupied when Harper had dropped Starling off, was overflowing with empty cars. The main entrance was emblazoned with a bald eagle, but there was nothing to signal there was life behind the predator-covered doors. The emptiness did nothing to comfort her nerves.

"Do you want me to go in with you?" Harper offered, trying to break the tense silence that filled every inch of their space.

Chance squeezed the steering wheel and then glanced, sideways, at her. "Why did you take her to school again?"

Not another fight.

"She wanted to say goodbye to her friends before you took her to God-knows-where." She stopped. She hadn't meant to escalate the situation. No. "I mean, I couldn't say no. She really seemed like she wanted to go to school."

"Did you ever stop to think no teenager ever wants to go to school?"

She sat back against the seat. "She wanted to go."

"Well, I guess we are about to find out why." His fingers uncurled from the wheel. He pulled the keys from the ignition and stuffed them into his pocket.

"We?"

"You got us into this mess. The least you can do is come help me figure a way out."

"I'm sorry, Chance." She reached down and opened up the door. "I didn't mean for anything like this to happen. I just wanted to help her out—I wanted to see her smile at least once."

"She's a teenage girl. Trying to see her smile is like trying to find Bigfoot. Some people swear it exists, but I doubt I'll ever see one."

Harper smiled as she thought of Chance sitting out in the woods looking for a Sasquatch. For a moment, just before he slammed his door shut, she could have sworn Chance's lips trembled into a thin smile, but as they made their way past the snatching claws of the eagle there were no traces.

They walked into the school's front office. In the back of the office, through the glass window of the principal's office, Harper noticed Starling sitting with her back to them.

The secretary behind the desk stood up. "Can I help you?" the woman asked in a way that made it clear they were more of an annoyance than they were welcome.

"Yes," Chance said, stepping into the no-fly zone of the battle, which promised to soon rage behind the closed doors of the principal's office. "I received a call saying my daughter ... Starling ... needed my help."

His help? Harper smiled. There was nothing sexier than a man taking a power position—unless the argument was with her.

The secretary glanced at the door and her face puckered into a tight scowl. "Yes, let me just call Principal Johnson and ask if he's ready to see you."

The woman punched the numbers into the phone and waited with her nose up in the air. The principal, who was sitting in the office with Starling, picked up the phone. The principal's bald head bobbed as he spoke.

"Ms. Jackson's father and ... his friend ... are here to see you." The secretary's voice was sticky sweet, a far contrast to the harsh edge she had given Chance and Harper.

He looked at them through the windows and waved them in.

Harper pushed past Chance, who was staring at the secretary.

"Yes, he can see you now," the secretary said, chasing after her.

"Thanks," Chance offered.

The secretary stepped in front of the door, stopping Harper in her tracks.

"Let me get that for you," the secretary said, sneering at her as if she took some level of joy out of opening the floodgates.

Chance led the way into the office. Principal Johnson stood up and extended his hand. "Nice to meet you. You are Starling's father, yes?"

"Name's Chance Landon." He nodded as he shook the man's hand.

The principal turned to Harper and stuck out his fat octopus hand. "And you are?"

"I'm Harper Cygnini. I'm a … " She thought about saying their friend, but she stopped. "They're staying with me for a bit."

The principal's eyebrows rose like two fat gray-speckled caterpillars as he looked at her with a mixture of disdain and confusion. "Well, please sit." The principal motioned to the two seats on either side of Starling. "I'm sorry we have to meet under these circumstances. I know Starling has been through a lot in the last week. Frankly, I was a bit surprised to see her return to school so quickly. No funeral plans for Carey?"

She tried to not notice Chance wince as they sat down in the offered chairs. "We have to wait for the autopsy to be complete before we can make plans."

"Ah. Well of course we all offer our deepest sympathies for your family's loss," the principal said in a flat voice. "That being said, I'm still not sure why you would put Starling through the ropes so soon after her mother's death."

"I thought it best if Starling got to say goodbye to her friends before she went on the road with me," Chance said as he leaned back into the chair.

Harper hadn't intended on sending Chance to slaughter—there was no way the bald principal with the much too tight tie was not going to judge the poker playing drifter.

The principal's brows crinkled, making the caterpillars scrunch together. What little light had been in his eyes disappeared.

"Actually," Harper said, trying to lessen the blow, "it was my idea to bring her. I wanted to talk to her—I was trying to get her to be my friend."

Starling jerked in her chair and for the first time, her eyes left the floor in front of the principal's desk. Her lips parted as if she wanted to say something, but she stopped and her gaze dropped back down to the ugly blue industrial strength carpet, which seemed to be in every school.

The principal seemed unwavering in his judgments. "It is nice you are trying to connect with Starling, but what she needs right now is a break. If you were accustomed to the needs of a young woman, you would have known she needs time—and a therapist. This is only made more evident by her behavior in the classroom."

Chance leaned forward. "What exactly happened?"

The principal looked toward Starling. "Do you want to tell them, Starling, or would you rather that I do?"

Starling didn't look up or answer; instead she merely shook her head.

"Well, I'm sorry to have to be the one to tell you." The pudgy man gave a weak nod as he glanced over at Chance. "But your daughter made a series of poor choices upon her arrival to the classroom this morning. As you know we, per school policy, have a no-tolerance stance on bullying type behaviors."

"You expect me to believe Starling bullied another student?" Chance said in disbelief.

"That's not what I said," Principal Johnson said in a clipped monotone voice. "If you'd allow me to finish, I was going to say Starling was a victim of a bullying incident which involved the throwing of her composition notebook."

Chance leaned forward until he had to put his hands on the principal's desk to keep from falling over. "Then why are we here if she was bullied?"

"Unfortunately, instead of telling a school official about the incident she decided to take matters into her own hands."

Harper tried not to smile.

"And?" Chance asked.

"She punched a young man in the face. We were forced to send him to the hospital as I believe she broke his nose."

Harper forced herself to look at the floor to cover her uncontrollable smile. Starling was a nymph—they were never the kind to let another person break them … or push them down. The boy was an idiot.

"Let me get this right," Chance said. "You are upset because my daughter defended herself when *she* was being bullied?"

"It doesn't stop there, Mr. Landon."

"What next? Are you going to expel her for hitting the bully?"

The principal leaned back in his chair. "Mr. Landon, not only did she hit the boy and send him to the hospital, but she also stole his cell phone and used it to make a call."

Harper finally gained control of her proud smile. It was one thing for Starling to defend herself, but it was another to steal. The girl had to have known she could use any phone she had wanted—there was no reason to take anything. Unless she hadn't wanted her or Chance to know she was making a call.

"Oh." Chance deflated. He turned to face the downtrodden Starling. "Who were you calling?"

Starling shrugged.

"You don't know? Or you don't want to tell me?"

Starling remained silent.

"So what are you telling us, Principal Johnson?" Harper asked, trying to take the pressure off the young woman.

"As I said, I think Starling should go to counseling to deal with the issues of her mother's passing and her residual anger issues."

What was he, some kind of psychologist? Harper tried to keep her anger in check. She was here to help. "I will see what I can do."

"In the meantime," the principal continued, "I think it would be best for her to take some time away from school. We are about to go on winter break in another week. Starling, I want you to take this week off. That way you can take two weeks to reflect on your actions and see how you can come back and make a positive change in your attitude and the environment around you."

Starling finally looked up. "So you're suspending me?"

The principal gave her a weak smile. "This is a unique set of circumstances, so I don't see the point in marring your permanent record." The man's caterpillar eyebrows scrunched together as he looked over at Harper and then Chance. "You are going to have a tough road to travel for the foreseeable future. You don't need this type of trouble added to the list."

"It doesn't really matter what goes on my record."

"She doesn't mean that," Chance said, stopping Starling from making another mistake.

Chapter Seventeen

Chance just couldn't make sense of all the whys in his life: why Harper had taken Starling to school, why Starling would have gone ape-shit when the kid threw her composition notebook, or why Starling had stolen a phone and made a mystery phone call. Chance had to get to the bottom of it. Unfortunately, he also had to be in Vegas.

How did most parents do it? How did they keep track of their kids and then have a normal life? What did they do when everything seemed to fall down around them?

He'd never felt so torn before. He needed to stay with Starling and help her deal with all the things going on in her life. They needed to connect; after the incident at school it was easy to see that she needed, more than anything, someone she could turn to—someone who would listen and help her get through this. Yet, he'd made a promise to Kodie to help him pay back Three-Eyed Nate—and it was one promise that couldn't be broken. Kodie's life was in danger.

He glanced across the front seat of the truck. Though they were all touching each other, but no one spoke almost as if they were afraid of the things that would be said.

"Starling," he said breaking the silence. "Is there anything you want talk about? I mean about why you did what you did?"

Starling stared out the window, not making eye contact with him.

"You know you can trust me with anything. I won't be upset." He sounded just like his own mother and for a passing second he felt guilty for all the trouble he had caused her when he'd been young. Not until now, surrounded by the weighted silence of a teenager, did he understand what his mother must have gone through when dealing with him. He sent a silent thank you up to the heavens.

Starling didn't budge.

Harper glanced over at him and shook her head, almost like she was begging him to stop. As much as he hated to admit it, Harper was right. He wasn't getting anywhere with Starling. The girl would have to open up on her own time. All he could do was wait. He could only be there.

Kodie was standing in the kitchen when they arrived back at Jenna's house. His head was stuck in the fridge as if he was trying to make food appear that wasn't there. What little groceries Chance had bought were already passing memories. Sitting on the kitchen table was the taped package of drugs they had pulled out of the bathroom wall. Chance rushed toward the package, but Starling reached it first. The girl picked up the block and turned it around in her hands.

She turned to face him. "Where did you get this?" she asked, almost as an accusation for some unknown crime.

"We just found the stuff. What do you know about it?"

Starling stuffed the brick of drugs under her arm. "You don't have any right going through my things."

Warning bells sounded in his mind. "Why would you have a brick of drugs?"

Starling glared at him, but said nothing and turned to run up the stairs.

"Stop. Right. There," he growled. "You aren't taking those drugs anywhere. You are going to sit here and talk to me until I know what the hell is going on. I can't handle any more of your silent treatment." His heartbeat thundered in his ears with his rising blood pressure.

Starling turned back. "You're an asshole. Anyone ever told you that?"

"You. Sit. Down." He pointed at the table that would serve as the courtroom.

Harper stared at him like he had just gone rabid. He wasn't backing down. He wasn't a great dad, but there was no way he was going to let his teenage daughter walk out of the room carrying illicit drugs. For once, he welcomed being called an asshole. It meant he was doing something right in the game of parenting.

The teenager stomped her feet as she moved to the table and plopped down in the chair.

"Set the drugs on the table and don't touch them again," Chance ordered.

Kodie slipped by him. "I'll be packing my stuff."

Chance answered with a tight nod.

"Do you know what is in that package?" Harper asked, pointing at the drugs in front of Starling.

"You guys already know, so why are you asking me?"

The hair on the back of his neck bristled. "We don't know. So why don't you inform us?" He tried to keep the anger from his voice, but that was one battle he couldn't win. All he'd done lately was fight—he was steadily moving past the ability for self-control. He shuddered to think of what the next night would bring—even if he was lucky, if he couldn't control his emotions he would be out of the game as soon as the poker tournament started.

"It's drugs," Starling said in a clipped voice.

"Are you a drug addict like your mother?"

"Carey wasn't a drug addict." Starling dropped her piercing gaze to the table. "Well, she was … but not like that. She wasn't a bad person."

Harper sat down across from Starling and, reaching out, took the teenager's hands. "If you are addicted to something we can get you the help you need to get over this. You just need to tell us the truth. We're here for you."

"I'm not a drug addict." Starling looked up to Harper. "Well, I guess I am, but I can't live with this."

"Live with what?" Harper said softly.

"I've been trying to ration my medicine. This was my last brick—I need it to last." Starling ran her finger along the end of the plastic square. "I can't control anything. I thought maybe I could get some more, but I can't … There's no hope. I can't live without my supply."

Was that what had been going on? His daughter had been going through detox? Was that why she had been so quiet, and so mercurial?

"Why didn't you tell me?" Chance stopped. Of course she wouldn't have told him, he who was barely above a stranger, that she had been addicted to drugs. He could hardly blame her. If she had told him this when she'd first stepped into his life, it was hard to say how he would have reacted, but there wasn't a doubt in his mind that he wouldn't have been standing in front of her. A sense of shame crept up his spine. He wasn't cut out for this whole *dad* thing. Starling deserved better. She deserved to have a father who could do better, be better.

"I never told anyone," Starling started. "Only Carey and Jenna knew about my condition … you know … connecting with spirits."

"Is that why you are doing drugs? So you can escape from your ability?" Harper asked.

"What?" Starling looked confused. "What are you talking about?" She paused for a second and stared down at the drugs in her hands. "Do you think this is like crack or something?"

Harper's cheeks took on a pink hue. "Uh, well … Isn't it?"

"No." Starling snorted. "My mother would've had a fit if she thought I was on those kinds of things."

Some of Chance's anger withered away. Was it possible Carey wasn't as bad as he had assumed?

"So what is this stuff?" He poked the package, sliding it a little closer to Starling.

"It's an anti-psychotic medication."

Chance had to stop his jaw from dropping. "What? Uh … " He didn't know how to respond. He wanted her to know he would always be there for her. He also didn't want her to think he felt sorry for her.

"What kind of anti-psychotic med? Is it one of the old ones or one of the new atypical drugs?" Harper asked.

"What? What's an atypical?" Chance felt like the last one to the party.

"Atypicals are a newer class of anti-psychotics. They don't have as many side effects as the older meds," Harper answered without so much as a blink of the eye.

The teen nodded, seeming to completely follow what Harper was saying, though Chance had no idea. "It's an older med. They started making it about twenty years ago, but it never made it through the clinical trials for FDA approval."

Harper bit her lip as if she was trying to keep back from saying something. After a moment her lips parted. "It didn't pass FDA approval? You aren't really taking this drug, are you?"

Starling nodded. "It is the only thing that works."

"From keeping you from going crazy?" Chance tried to reel the words back in, but they had already spewed past his lips.

"Is that what you think?" Starling glared at him. "I'm crazy?"

"That's not what I meant. I just don't understand, that's all. You have to be patient with me."

"What the hell do you think I've been doing?" Starling rebuked.

"Stop," Harper said, putting her hands up. "I don't think your dad's trying to imply anything. Like he said, he just doesn't understand."

"Exactly, Starling. I just want to be able to figure out what is going on with you—so I can help." Chance gave Harper a look of thanks.

"If you want to help, you need to find Dr. Eliot McDougal. He used to sell Jenna and Carey the drugs, but he won't sell me any. I tried to call him today, but he wouldn't answer. I don't know what I'm going to do."

If the doctor was some piece of trash who took advantage of Jenna, Chance's daughter, and his ex-wife by selling them drugs there would be hell to pay. He had to hope the doctor only had the purest of intentions in mind when he sold Carey drugs that hadn't passed FDA approval. God only knew what side effects the drugs would have on his daughter—or why the drug had failed testing.

"Starling, I feel like I need to tell you that these aren't the drugs you brought with you. We never searched through your things. We came across this package here in Jenna's house. So you have whatever you have in your bag and now this. But before I give you this I want to know something." Harper stared down at the innocuous looking brown package. "What happens if you don't take the drugs?"

"I see more and more spirits." The teen sucked in a breath. "The last time I was without my meds was a few years ago. It only took two weeks before I couldn't get out of bed. When I don't take my medication, the spirits become too much—the only place I can escape is in my sleep or my shift. Even then ... sometimes they try to invade my mind ... I need this. I can't survive in a world full of spirits—not all of them are good." Starling pulled the package into her chest like a precious possession.

"Did that have something to do with the incident at school today?" Chance forced himself to mimic Harper's soft tone.

His daughter looked up at him and there were tears at the corners of her eyes. "I didn't mean to lose my temper. My mom was there. She wanted to come through. She wanted me to write something. I haven't talked to her much since she died. I started letting her in, but before she could tell me anything, the boy took my notebook. I don't know what happened. The next thing I knew, I had blood dripping off my knuckles." Her voice cracked and a tear slipped down her soft childlike cheek. "I'm so sorry. I don't mean to be like this. I just … I just can't help it."

His heart lurched and he kneeled down next to his heartbroken daughter. Reaching up, he wiped away the tear from her cheek. "Don't cry, sweetheart. This isn't your fault. You can't control what is going on inside of you any more than you can control a river."

Her beautiful brown eyes sparkled with unspent tears. "I'm not the person you must think I am."

"I hope you are the girl I know you to be. You're smart. Mysterious. You're brave. I only just met you and I already love you with all my heart. You are my daughter. My child. I never thought I would be this lucky. We'll do whatever we need to do to get you what you need."

• • •

There was a steady stream of cars leaving Vegas. Their headlights lit up the night as the winners and the losers escaped what many called the den of sin, but what Harper merely thought of as a place for escape. For the next few days, her only goal would be to find Dr. McDougal and talk to him about getting more of the medication for Starling. If she found him, she could learn more about the drug and why it hadn't passed federal testing. From there, maybe—just maybe—she could figure out what it was about the compound that acted as a buffer between Starling and the spirit world.

She would need to go about investigating without drawing attention to herself or what she was doing. If word got back to

Merckson that she was sniffing around Shaw she'd undoubtedly come under fire. She would have to kiss her job goodbye. Her job was everything. Or at least it had been.

Over the last few days something had changed. Suddenly she wasn't just living for herself anymore—and as much as she had originally been uncomfortable with their arrangement, it was starting to grow on her. The more time she spent with Chance and Starling, the more it began to seem like they had slipped into the roles of a family.

The truck bumped down the highway as Chance yawned from behind the steering wheel. Harper looked into the backseat of the cab. Starling's eyes were shut and her chest rose and fell in the constant rhythm that came with sleep brought on through emotional exhaustion. Kodie had his head planted against the back window; his gold crown sparkled as another car passed by, casting light into his gaping mouth.

Harper turned back to Chance. "What are you going to do?"

He glanced over at her for a second, but then stared back at the road. "About what?"

"The drugs. Are you going to let her keep taking them?"

"I'm going to have to let her. They're the only thing helping her. She needs them."

"You do understand if the FDA didn't approve these drugs, there's something terribly wrong with them, don't you?"

He glanced in the rearview mirror toward his sleeping daughter. "I know … but she's a nymph, right? The drugs must not have the same effects as they would on a regular human, right?"

The memory of Jenna's funeral sprang into her mind. For a moment, all she could see was the Chief Medical Examiner, Dr. Redbird, standing in front of her with her mousy brown hair and beaky nose, wanting to talk about Jenna's demise. "Even we can die."

"So you think these drugs are going to kill her?"

"Very few drugs out there can kill us, but there are a few—anything that makes us lose our hair or our feathers. All I'm saying is it would be best if we knew exactly what it is Starling is taking and who the doctor is who was giving it to her."

"Didn't you say this Shaw Pharmaceuticals is located in Vegas?" His fingers curled tight on the steering wheel.

"I was already thinking about that. When you start the tournament, I can find the company. Maybe I can pull some strings and meet Dr. McDougal. Maybe he'll talk to me—I already know what he's trying to hide. He won't have another choice but to explain himself to me." She tried to sound optimistic, but the sound fell flat. There were so many things that could go wrong. Heck, she'd be lucky to make it through the door of their facility. There was a rivalry between Merckson and Shaw—each had their share of secrets.

"What happens if he doesn't talk to you?"

"Then we'll have to hope and pray my company can figure out what drug Starling is taking, or else maybe we can try to find a replacement for her—something else that can help her get a handle on the spirits."

The air stilled between them and the cars continued to flash by. In the distance, thousands of lights lit up the sky as Las Vegas came into view—an oasis of light in a lonesome desert.

Maybe she could appeal to McDougal's softer side, convince him she needed to know the truth in order to save Starling's life. Yet, as she thought about why the man would become involved with a nymph and her spiritually connected daughter, the less it seemed like appealing to his sensitivity would work. If he were anything like the men she worked with, he would be all business and driven by the ruler of capitalism—money.

Why did everything have to come down to money? Money had driven the men who had killed Jenna. Money had driven Kodie to be so desperate to take a loan out from a hustler. Greed was the reason they were coming here.

And then it struck her. She wasn't all that different from the man who had sold Carey the drugs. There she was, only caring about getting back to work—to make more money. Money she didn't really need, but was willing to give up relationships in order to get. She'd been so centered on her work for so long she'd forgotten all the things that were really important in her life—and her complacency had inadvertently caused her sister's death. No matter how much money passed through her hands, it would never cleanse her hands of blood.

Kodie's soft open-mouthed snores stopped as they made their way onto the Strip. To their left was a line of black limousines. The windows were tinted, hiding the parties that must have been going on inside. A yawn escaped from the back as Starling shuffled in her seat.

A valet stood outside of the Bellagio as they pulled up to the stand. When the man stepped up to the door Harper noticed the deep bags under his eyes and she glanced down at her watch. Seven A.M. It was going to be a long day.

The valet opened the door. "Hello, and welcome to the Bellagio."

She stepped out with the help of the valet, who then made his way back to Starling's door. A strange, pinched expression covered Starling's face as she stared at the man in the suit jacket. She stepped out, not taking his offered hand. There was something wrong.

"Starling, you okay?" Harper whispered as the young woman stepped next to her and waited for the men to come around to the sidewalk.

"I'm okay."

"Why didn't you like the valet?"

The driver's side doors of the truck closed with a slam.

"He looked like the boy who stole my notebook."

"Don't worry," Harper whispered. "You'll be okay. I'll take care of you."

Walking around the front of the truck, Chance palmed the man a bill as valet handed him his parking stub. With a wave, Harper motioned that she and Starling were going inside. Chance acknowledged her with a curt nod.

She'd forgotten how anything and everything in this city was bought with a smile and a cash-weighted handshake. It was a system she simultaneously loved and hated. There was a simplicity to it that was almost admirable. With enough money any secret could have been buried, but for only slightly more, any secret could have been bought—all one needed was a prolific bankroll and the right questions.

Greek statues stood guard at the doors that led into the grand hotel's gold and marble laden lobby. Light streamed through the collection of hand blown glass sculptures adorning the lobby's roof, casting a shimmering dance of colors across the pale marble floors.

The lobby was quiet with the exception of a group of men in black suits. One of the men had his blue tie off; at some point in the night he must have slung it over his shoulder and had forgotten it was there. His hair was disheveled and, as they walked toward them and the front desk, she noticed the thin veil of glitter plastered over the back of his expensive looking jacket. The man turned as she approached and he gave her a drunken smile. One of his blond friends listed and whispered loudly but unintelligibly into the ear of the man to his left.

"Hey ladies ... " the drunken man with the jacket covered in body glitter called. "If you girls are looking for some real men instead of those puny motherfuckers you're with ... " He pointed out the glass doors where Kodie and Chance were standing with the valet. "You can come right over." The peal of laughter echoed in the empty marble lobby.

Starling looked over to Harper with fear in her eyes.

"Don't worry," Harper said, trying to comfort the young girl. "Why don't you go with your dad and Kodie? I'll be right along."

Starling turned around and walked outside.

"Hiya, boys," Harper said in her best voice of seduction. The ripples of her nymph magic vibrated the air around her and she could see the waves overtake the men as she neared. "You're all *so* handsome. Do your wives know where you are?"

The glittered man's mouth fell open as he stared at her with what could have been best described as desperate fuck-me eyes. "I'm … I'm … " the man stammered. "I'm getting married this weekend."

"Oh really?" She smiled and stepped close. "What about the rest of you?"

The blond man who had whispered to his friend shook his head and his hair fell back slightly, exposing his receding hairline. "Our wives don't need to know *anything*. You know the saying … *What happens in Vegas stays in Vegas.*"

"I don't think it always does … " She gave half a laugh. "I'm known for doing things that leave an impression."

"I bet you've done a few things," the blond continued. "But you have never had a man as good as me. I'd fuck you so hard you wouldn't walk right for a week." He reached down and humped the air as if the trashy gesture was some kind of mating call.

"Only a week?" A wicked grin took over her lips. "I've been known to fuck so well that men could never walk again."

The blond's jaw dropped, but he quickly collected himself. "Prove it."

"Hand me your phone and I will," she said, stepping close enough to catch the scent of fading coconut body oil that must have been left over from their night at the strip club.

"Why do you need my cell?"

Harper let a surge of energy pass through her toward the man and his eyes glazed over. Perfect. "No pictures." She wiggled her finger and the other men in the small circle laughed.

The man dug in his back pocket and handed her his white cell phone. She tapped the buttons and opened up the screen. There was a picture of a half-naked woman spread over the back of a motorcycle as his wallpaper. If she had to guess he must not have been getting much play at home, but from the state of the drunken, coconut-smelling man at her side, she could hardly blame his wife.

Clicking open his pictures, buried deep in the files, she found a picture of a mousy woman with sad eyes. She had to be his wife. The woman reminded her of an abused dog, slouching as if she was just waiting for another blow.

If the poor woman would have been some sumptuous egocentric looking woman, Harper would have snapped a picture of herself and sent the woman a text message with the words, "Your husband is a pig" embedded. Yet, after seeing the picture of the meek woman, it didn't seem right. The poor woman probably had more than she could handle in her philandering husband.

Instead she opened up the internet and found an app for gay men and downloaded it to his phone. The phone opened to a menu entitled: "What kind of man do you wish to meet?" She laughed as she typed: "Wanted: one good man … Preferably denim clad Dom with ample assets for play. I'm shy. Cameras welcome."

With a flick of the wrist, she dropped the homosexual homing beckon into the man's pocket. She giggled as she imagined his next experience in the men's bathroom in the massive hotel.

The doors to the lobby opened and she turned as Kodie, Chance, and Starling made a beeline to her and the group of men.

"Have a good night, boys." She gave a little wave of the fingers as she stepped away from the group.

"Wait … " the drunken man called after her as she strode toward Chance.

"What in the hell is going on? Starling told me—" Chance started.

"Don't worry about it," she answered with a mischievous grin. "I took care of them."

"What did you do?" Kodie asked.

Her smile grew wider. "If I were you, I would avoid being near him unless you are interested in meeting one *good* man."

She grabbed Chance's arm and steered him away from the drunken men, but he kept looking back over his shoulder toward the pigs. "Are you sure you don't need me to talk to them?"

"Trust me on this. I've been dealing with men longer than you've been one."

Kodie snickered.

The woman behind the massive welcome desk smiled as they made their way over to her. "Hello, and welcome to the Bellagio. How can I help you this morning?" Her voice was robotically chipper as if all humanness had long ago seeped out of the gold-plated machine that was the hotel.

Chance stepped forward and pulled his wallet from his pocket. "I have a reservation for a two room suite under the name Chance Landon."

He was met with a tap of keys as the woman put his name into the computer. "Oh yes, Mr. Landon, it says here you are playing in the Champions of Poker Tournament. As a thank you for your participation in such a prestigious event we have upgraded your suite to the penthouse and also compensated you for your room. If you need anything, please do not hesitate to let us know. All of your incidentals will be on the house."

"I guess I only have one question, and that's about my daughter. She's not quite eighteen. She was hoping to watch the tournament, would it be okay?"

"As you are a VIP guest we will make an exception, sir. However, she must not stand too close to the gaming tables and she must be accompanied by an adult."

"Not a problem." Chance slid his wallet back down into his pocket. "Thank you." The words came out almost as if they were a question.

"It's the Bellagio's pleasure, sir. We are honored to have you staying as one of our guests."

As long as Harper had been alive, she'd never been treated like a famous person. She'd never had a room comped, even when she'd gone to pharmaceutical conventions. Up until this moment she'd never really thought of Chance as famous, but as the woman across the desk finally broke her robotic demeanor and gave Chance a provocative smile, she could no longer be blind to his reality. No wonder he hadn't wanted to quit the game, to start living a life devoted to a child. He may have been a drifter by definition, but there was so much more—so much she didn't know.

A strange sadness filled her. Until now, she'd thought she understood him and what made him tick. Had she been wrong all along? She glanced over at him and noticed the way his strong jaw made an elegant line as it melded into the tanned flesh of his neck. A neck that only a handful of hours ago she'd been kissing. Heat permeated from her core.

The woman's dangerous smile fell from her lips as she glanced to Harper then down at her computer screen. "Also, Mr. Landon, it looks as though you have someone waiting for you in the penthouse."

"You allowed someone into my room?" Chance growled.

"Sir, it says here that he is a friend of the casino floor manager. The man was not to be dissuaded." Smiling, as if she hadn't just told them all there was a stranger in their room, the clerk pushed four room keys into a small folder and handed it to Chance. The woman's fingers trembled as she stared up at Chance's face. "May you take the others in the tournament to the mattress, sir."

Harper chuckled. The only mattress the woman cared about was one she hoped to share with Harper's man. She stepped forward and slipped her arm through the crook of Chance's. "Oh, I'm sure he will. Mr. Landon isn't the kind of man to be underestimated."

Chapter Eighteen

A vase sat on the dining room table at the center of the penthouse suite. A bouquet of white, hopeful lilies reached out like begging hands—but there was no hope to be found in the room—at least not now. Not when, in the adjoining living room, two men waited in overstuffed lounge chairs. Each man wore a black suit and neither wore a smile. The younger man, with brown hair bordering on black, scanned the room constantly and his body was at full attention, standing guard over the gentleman with the silver threaded hair. Something about the pair reminded Harper of guidos from the Italian mafia.

"Sir, they are here," the bodyguard said, dropping his hand to his hip where he must have been carrying a weapon.

The stoic gray-haired man turned as the small group of road worn travelers walked into the living room.

"Chance Landon?" The gray-haired man stood up and extended his hand, but the simple action was performed with the formality of a state meeting.

"Yes. And you are?" Chance stared at the man's hand for a moment and then stepped forward and gave it a stern shake.

"I'm Mr. Blackwater, the gaming commissioner here in Vegas."

Recognition flickered on Chance's face. Kodie stepped back and behind Harper, as if all of a sudden he no longer wanted to be standing in the room.

"It's nice to meet you, sir." Chance motioned to the chair. "Please sit."

"We aren't planning on staying long. We just needed to have a quick meeting with you, preferably without your associates."

Harper glanced over at Chance and there was a look of mild terror on his face—like a man facing the executioner. What had he gotten himself into? What wasn't he telling her? Why would the gaming commissioner want to see Chance the moment he arrived in Las Vegas?

The man's bodyguard stepped toward Chance and whispered something in his ear. A trace of terror rippled over his features, but was replaced by an impassive front. His terror was disconcerting—when he, a poker player, let his emotions slip, all that she could be certain of was that it was something unusual, something terrifying. Yet his cold impenetrability was far more disconcerting than his fear.

"Why don't you and Starling run to the lab and see if you can find Dr. McDougal? I'm going to need to handle a few things before the tournament begins."

"Are you sure?" she asked, trying to ignore the mixture of angst, concern, and fear for Chance. She already knew what his answer would be, but her protectiveness for him wouldn't allow her to walk away without attempting to stay.

"Yes," Chance said with a stiff nod. "I'll be fine." His gaze flickered to the bodyguard's gun-laden hip. "Here." He pulled the parking stub from his pocket and handed it to Harper.

She stuffed the stub into her purse, but she stared at the bodyguard's hand, which rested on the lump under his suit jacket.

There was no way he would let Harper and Starling stay, and there was nothing she could do about it—except hope she could find an ally in Kodie. She turned to him. "Kodie, we don't need you to come with us. Why don't you stay here with Chance?"

The bodyguard stepped toward her, but Mr. Blackwater stopped him with a wave of the hand. "Yes, Kodie can stay, but under the condition he stands outside of the door while we discuss our business."

At the very least Kodie would be there if anything got out of line. She glanced at Kodie and he gave her a small acknowledging nod. "Fine."

"Let's go, Starling," she said, leading the teen from the penthouse. The door closed behind them with an isolating, fearful thud, which paralleled the feeling in her stomach. She hated leaving Chance there to face the commissioner alone. She stared at the gold number plate next to the door. All that glittered most certainly was not gold. Everything about this tournament was tainted through greed, fear, and secrets—and she had the feeling there were more secrets that would be exposed long before the final card was played.

She and Starling made their way to the elevator bank and silently waited. Finally the door opened, but Harper hesitated—as soon as she left, there would be no way she could help Chance. Everything that happened to him would be out of her control.

The elevator dinged, she stepped into the empty car, and the doors slid shut behind them.

"Harper?" Starling asked.

"Hmm?"

"I know I told Chance he was an asshole and everything, but do you think he's going to be okay?"

How had she forgotten that she wasn't alone in her fears about Chance being in harm's way? She needed to stay strong. She may not have been able to control what was happening to Chance or to protect him, but she could protect his daughter.

"He's going to be fine. I'm sure they always have to meet with the gaming commissioner before these big tournaments. I'm sure there are a lot of things they have to talk about before the game."

Starling gave her a sideways glance. "Really?"

Harper forced herself to smile. "Absolutely." When Jenna had been alive she would have seen right through Harper's lie. The only time she ever said "absolutely" was when she wasn't sure or when she was extremely nervous—and usually they were simultaneous occurrences.

"Aren't you worried?"

"Absolutely not," she said with a forced nonchalance.

"What about us? Do you think we are going to be able to find Dr. McDougal?"

"We'll try." Her gut told her no, but if she was telling one or two lies she might as well keep going.

They made their way out into the lobby, which had started to fill with a few tourists that, from their excited on-the-top-of-the-world energy, had just arrived. It would have been nice to feel the same enthusiasm, the same level of excitement that everything would turn out great—that they would all come away from this place as winners. No matter how deep Harper searched her soul, she couldn't find anything close to excitement—she found fear, but buried even deeper there was an almost imperceptible flicker of hope. That tiny bit of blind hope would have to carry them through for a while. This was all out of her control—and maybe that fact, the uncontrollability, was what she feared the most.

The concierge smiled at them and made his way over. "May I help you, ladies?"

"Yes," Harper said with her overworked smile. "Do you know where I can find Shaw Pharmaceuticals?"

"Is there something you are in need of?" His gaze flickered to Starling and back to her. "I may be able to send someone out … for *anything* you may need."

Of course he must have thought they were looking to score drugs—Vegas through and through.

"Never mind. We just need our truck." She pulled the parking stub and a twenty from her purse and handed them to the man. The man smiled, but she couldn't help but wonder if he was used to getting a larger tip.

The man snapped his fingers and waved at a white-jacketed man who waited by the door, his hands behind his back in the long practiced position of those in servitude. The man in the white jacket hurried over. "Yes, sir. How may I help you?"

Without a word, the concierge handed the ticket to the man and pointed toward the door. The man scurried off.

While they waited, Harper tapped away on her smart phone until she found the driving directions and a photograph of the building. The labs were in a single-story building and, from the bird's-eye view, she could just make out a pretty little courtyard filled with trees at the building's center.

A crowd of tourists burst through the doors, black luggage in hand and enthusiastic smiles on their faces. Without watching where she was going as she headed toward the doors, Harper took one more look at her phone and stuffed it into her purse. Her shoulder connected with someone. She looked up and into the sneering face of a buttermilk-white tourist. "Watch where you're going," the woman growled.

Harper tried to resist the urge to say something, but Starling lunged forward. "You could have stepped out of the way, lady."

"Starling, no." Harper tried to warn her off. "I'm sorry. I wasn't watching."

"Damn right you're sorry. You're one dumb bitch. I mean just look at you." The tourist pointed at Starling. The woman's red lipstick cracked on her lips as she gave the teen a dangerous smile. "What in the hell do you think you are doing here, girl? Doesn't your mother know better than to bring a *child* into a casino?"

Harper bristled, but there was no sense in fighting with the milky tourist.

"I'm not a child." Starling fumed.

"Starling, let's go." Harper pointed through the doors, toward their waiting truck. "This isn't worth the fight. We have more important things to worry about ... please."

Starling glanced over at her and some of the anger seemed to escape her eyes. The shrill woman's laughter followed them as they walked away.

"Why didn't you say something?" Starling asked.

The valet walked over to them and handed Harper the keys to Chance's pickup truck. The array of keys weighed heavy in Harper's hand as she gave the valet the almost required tip. "Starling, there are some things that are worth fighting for and there are times when you are only wasting your breath. That woman didn't matter. It didn't matter what she said or did, it is in the past and there is no changing it with a fight."

"You don't think you should have stood up for us—for me?"

"When it matters, I'll stand up for you. I'll protect you, just like Chance will." Pain radiated through her hand as she gripped the keys tighter.

"She called me a child."

The valet opened Starling's door and motioned for her to enter. Starling stared at Harper as she stepped up into the passenger seat and then pulled the composition book from her bag.

"You're not a child, but there are so many things you are going to learn. One of those things is learning when to stand up and fight and when to walk away."

The valet closed Starling's door and Harper followed him around to her side. "Thank you," Harper said with a smile as the man opened her door and she stepped up and into the driver's seat.

The truck's engine roared to life. Had she been wrong in not standing up for Starling? Should she have gone farther in the confrontation with the woman? Maybe. She replayed the woman's words in her mind and she tried to imagine how it would have gone if she hadn't made them leave—each time she imagined the argument, it ended badly—so there had been no other choice.

Shifting gears, Harper pushed the truck into first and drove out of the long driveway and onto the back roads, which led out of the hotel—and farther from Chance.

There were so many other things to be concerned with— Chance and Kodie were up in the penthouse with a man Harper wasn't sure they could trust, there was still a death that had left them all with questions, and Starling needed her medication. They had more important battles coming. And the only thing she could control right now, the only battle they could fight and have any chance of winning, was finding Dr. McDougal and getting more of Starling's medication.

Even this battle wasn't one they were likely to win, but this was one that was worth the fight. Harper hated the thought of telling Starling the ugly truth—that the chances were low she would be able to help Starling. If Dr. McDougal hadn't wanted to talk to Starling, there was only a thin chance he would allow a rival lab rat to enter his sanctum in search of information and more drugs.

Harper's phone chirped from her purse. Somewhat relieved to have some type of escape from Starling's festering silence, Harper pulled the phone from her purse and pressed it to her ear. "Hello?" She pulled the truck to a stop at a red light.

"Hi." She was met with a familiar voice. "Is this Harper Cygnini?"

"Yes, it is. How can I … " She stopped herself. The robotic hotel staff's words refused to leave her lips. "Yes?"

"This is Ariadne Papadakis. From Crete?"

What was the leader of the sisterhood of Epione doing calling her? Her body tensed.

"Yes. Hi, Ms. Papadakis. How are you?"

"You can call me Ariadne—we're sisters. And I'm … okay." There was a long pause. "Actually. I'm calling with a bit of a problem."

"A problem? What kind of problem?"

Ariadne cleared her throat. "Well … After your sister's death and the recent increase of nymph deaths we, the sisterhood was forced to launch an investigation. We believe there are more to the deaths than a simple rancher in Montana wanting to hybrid his rodeo stock. There's something else going on we have yet to completely understand. So, in an effort to find out the truth, we have had a man, Jasper Gray, watching you and your friends."

A man had been watching them? A man sent by the sisterhood? Chills rippled down her spine. Why hadn't she thought of this? Of course the sisterhood would want to learn more about the nymph deaths—especially after Carey had been killed and there were no suspects in custody.

Harper glanced over at the young woman. Starling mumbled something and her pen moved in the strange rhythmic motions that came with one of her automatic writing sessions. The familiar word *Red* started to fill the white paper.

The phone line was quiet. "Harper?" Ariadne finally asked. "Are you still there?"

"Yes, I'm here." The light turned green and Harper drove with the traffic. "Since you are watching us, you know who I'm with and what we're doing, yes?"

"Yes, we know you are in Vegas. Jasper's staying in the Bellagio, keeping an eye on you and your comrades."

"Is he following us now?" Harper peered into her rear view mirror, but was met with a countless number of cars.

"It's hard to say. He might be. We assigned him to watch out for you and your safety."

"Do you think we're in danger?"

There was a momentary pause. "We're going to take all the precautions we can. We would hate to lose any more of our kind. We've lost so many wonderful women of late. If we continue losing nymphs at this rate—we may well not come back. You know our birth rates—Starling is the first nymph born in the last century and she may well be the last."

Between the curse of their kind and the impossibility of getting pregnant without entering the blessed river, Ariadne was right. They had to be concerned. There weren't many of their species left.

"Who do you think is behind Carey's death?"

"At this point we aren't sure, but we have a lead … That's why I'm calling."

"What do you mean?" Harper asked. "You don't think I had something to do with it do you?"

"No, but we have reason to believe that these deaths are all connected—including your sister's and Carey's."

"But they found Jenna's killers. They're in jail in Montana, remember?"

"Yes, her killers are. But we think this all has to do with fertility—Carey was the only nymph who'd given birth since the late 1800s when Trina, one of the Cretan nymphs, was born."

"Why would someone want to kill Carey for being fertile?" Harper tried to understand, but none of this made any sense.

"We're not sure why they would have wanted to kill her, but we think there are others who are trying to understand Carey's pregnancy and her ability to have a child … other supernatural beings like us … like the nymphs."

"Do you think they are going to come after Chance?" Harper made her way over to the side of the road and pulled to a stop.

Starling jerked to attention. "What's going on, Harper?"

Harper lifted her finger, gesturing for the girl to wait.

"We think they may be targeting him too, but he has luck on his side. There are only a few who are privy to who and what the father of the child is."

"That's good … " There was a slight sense of relief—at least Chance was safe—for now. "What about Starling?"

The teen stared at her. Her pen was still to the paper, but she had stopped writing.

"Is Starling safe?"

"Well … " Ariadne paused. "I don't think so. After you all left last night, your sister's house was broken into. Our man was following you and wasn't there when it happened. We only found out this morning."

"What? Who would want to break into the house?"

"We think they were looking for something," Ariadne answered. "Do you have any idea what they would have been looking for?"

The drugs … Harper didn't know whether to admit to the find or not. "Do you know who might be behind the break in?" Harper changed the subject.

"We aren't sure yet, but your neighbors reported seeing a small brunette woman at your house in the early morning hours. Do you know what she would have been looking for?"

"We found drugs in the house." Harper gripped the steering wheel tight. "We dumped most of them."

"You did what?" Starling dropped her composition book on the floorboard of the truck. "But … I need those … "

Harper covered her phone. "I know, sweetheart. We dumped them before we knew."

Starling gave her a sideways glance as if she couldn't believe her.

"What kind of drugs were they? Do you know?" Ariadne continued, unaware of the look of disgust and anguish on Starling's face.

Harper reached over and took Starling's hand and gave it a light, reassuring squeeze. "They're an anti-psychotic that failed clinical testing."

"Is that all the drug is used for?"

Starling shook her head, as if telling her not to expose her ability to a stranger. Harper paused. Telling Ariadne that Starling needed help to control the spirits was not her secret to tell. "I'm not really sure."

"Did you find the drugs anywhere else besides your sister's house?"

"Carey had some."

"I see," Ariadne said, her voice pensive. "Because of the events that have transpired recently, I need you to stop the drugs from getting into anyone else's hands."

"I will," Harper answered.

"And please find out as much as you can about the drug. I have a feeling that there is more to this drug, something that would make supernaturals desperate enough to kill to get their hands on it. "

"We'll get everything we can from Shaw Laboratories."

"Great. And please make sure to stay safe. I can't guarantee whoever it was that was in your home won't slip by Jasper. And we don't want any more nymphs getting hurt."

Chapter Nineteen

The khaki-colored doors in front of Harper and Starling acted as a barrier to the world—on one side were questions and the other side answers. Harper could almost feel the potential behind them, if only they could get entrance into the laboratory. She pressed the doorbell attached to the little black speaker, which led to some unknown receptionist in some unknown room behind the pale, unwelcoming doors.

"Shaw Laboratories, may I see your ID?" The woman's voice, distorted by static and grainy interference, echoed out into the concrete entrance.

Above them was a black camera with a red dot. They were watching. Digging through her purse, she pulled out her ID and lifted it toward the camera, so the unknown woman could judge her worthy of admittance. Starling followed suit.

"Harper Cygnine … Cygnini," the woman behind the microphone stumbled over her name. "May I ask why you have come to see us today?"

Harper paused for a moment. Should she go under the veil of her title or should she play the card of innocent intent—acting as if she only wished to meet Dr. Eliot McDougal? There would be no way they would open the doors to a rival, but they also wouldn't let just anyone in off the street.

"I was hoping to talk to Dr. Eliot McDougal. Is there any way I could come in and speak to him, concerning his work?"

There was a long pause behind the microphone. "What exactly are you wishing to speak to him about?"

"I'm a pharmacologist from Merckson and I have a great deal of admiration for his work with his new compounds. I'm looking for a new job and I thought perhaps he would be willing to see me concerning a lab position."

There was another long pause as Harper assumed the woman talked to Dr. McDougal. "I'm sorry. Dr. McDougal is not taking visitors."

Shit.

Harper turned and followed Starling into the parking lot. What were they going to do? She chastised herself for not having a better plan—of course a rival company wasn't going to allow two strangers in from off the street. They would have to come up with another way to get what they needed.

"It'll be okay, Starling." Harper stared up at the flat face of the building as she opened the truck's door. "We just need to get in and ask a few questions. He won't say no if we are talking to him face-to-face."

"I wouldn't be so sure," Starling answered. "They wouldn't even let us in."

To be honest, Harper wasn't sure either, but there was no way she was going to let Starling down, not again—they had to get in.

"Wait," Harper said, as Starling moved to step up into the passenger side of the truck. "You said you've shifted before, right?"

"Absolutely." Starling nodded, but looked at Harper like she was losing her mind. "But wait, how are we going to get in as swans?"

"Look," Harper said, pointing at the top of a maple that poked up out of the center of the single-story building. "I think the building is built around a courtyard. We can shift and fly into the square. If we get lucky, we can sneak in to the building from there."

"Awesome."

Harper tried to not act shocked when a tight smile magically appeared on the normally sullen teen's lips. It was so nice to see the girl smile Harper almost forgot why she was smiling. "I … You … " Harper stammered. "Do you like to shift?"

"It's one of my favorite things, but it's been a long time. My mother hated when I shifted. You know … She was always telling me how dangerous it was—how if I have more than a single feather plucked I'll die."

Harper had misjudged Carey. She had thought Starling's mom had been nothing more than a drug addict, only caring about herself and where she could get her next hit, but she had never been more wrong. Yes, Carey had been using drugs, but not for recreation. Instead the drugs had been a necessity, not only for herself but for her daughter as well. Carey had loved Starling. Carey had done everything she could to help her daughter—and for all Harper knew, it was Carey's sacrifices that may have caused her death.

"Your mother was only trying to protect you from your shift?"

"Yes, but my shift is a nice break from having to deal with the spirits. It's the only time they don't bother me. It's like when I'm a bird I don't have to feel them there."

The love of shifting and the fear of doing so was something with which Harper could relate, but the realization that her mortality was in question had only occurred after Jenna's death. Never before had she been more frightened—her vulnerability, her soft underbelly, had been attacked. But it was different for Starling. Carey, her mother, had been overly protective and had wanted to save her daughter from the possible consequences of Starling's swan shift. She had wanted to protect her child and keep her safe—Carey's efforts had succeeded … and it only made it more clear how much Harper had failed Jenna.

"Well, you don't have anything to worry about. I promise I'll do everything I can to keep you safe." Harper meant what she said, but the nagging feeling of failure seeped into her thoughts and she couldn't help but wonder if she would fail this young woman just as she had failed Jenna.

"I trust you. Let's do this." Starling smiled again, this time her teeth gleamed in the waning winter sun.

A sliver of Harper's heart, a piece that had been missing after Jenna's death, clicked back into place. If Starling trusted her with her safety, Harper wouldn't let her down. She wouldn't let anyone hurt the beautiful raven-haired woman. "I think you should stay here."

"What?" Starling's delicate smile disappeared. "No. Didn't you tell me I needed to know when to walk away and when to fight? Well, this is my fight. I'm not staying here while you fight. I'm helping. You can't keep me away."

The young woman's bravery was commendable and her point unarguable. Starling had every right to fight her fight, but Harper would have to protect her every step of the battle. "Don't you think you will be safer here?"

"Yes, but that's not the issue." Starling paused. "Besides, we won't be in our swan form long, right? Plus, who would try to kill two swans inside a laboratory's courtyard?"

Starling had a point. These were the types who lived inside their work stations most of the day and then lived behind the computer for the rest.

"We can't be seen, Starling. If we fly in, we have to do so without being noticed. Okay?"

The teenager gave a begrudging shrug. "Alright, if you say so."

Checking to make sure no one was watching, Harper led Starling around the side of a warehouse building to the right of the lab. "Ready? Remember, no one can see us. We need to be careful."

"Got it."

Stripping down, Harper let the familiar, but seldom used, energy of her shift flutter through her body. The wonderful current was like a warm bath, soothing her frayed nerves and calming her with its waves. Her neck lengthened, but there was no pain, only a slight light-headed feeling as her body morphed. A soft wind blew down the stark alley between the warehouse and the lab and gently rustled the white feathers of her wings. She longed to catch the soft breeze and climb up into the skies and away from all the problems they were facing, but she'd never run away.

Starling's young curves melded into a familiar swan shape beside her. It stunned Harper to watch the way the young woman's eyes gleamed with excitement as she shifted. Her long black locks started to morph and change into beautiful black feathers, which sprouted and grew over her entire form. Her feathers caught a beam of sunlight and shone with a rich black so complicated with colors it appeared blue and then a brilliant red, reminding Harper of a prism the way the silken feathers captured the light and spread the colors like rays of hope. Harper gasped at Starling's inexplicable and unexpected beauty, but the gasp came out as a strange strangled breath.

With a quick motion of her head, Harper unfurled her wings and rose up into the sky. For a brief moment, she forgot why they had shifted as she concentrated on the touch of the wind. The breeze lifted her up like invisible hands and pulled her into the bosom of freedom. The fresh air filled her lungs with each pump of her wings. The rare black swan to her left lifted higher, and Harper raced to catch up.

The air current shifted as it swirled over the building, pulling her back down to earth and to the task at hand. For too long, both Harper and Starling had lived in the pressure cooker of their lives—for what? Starling was forced to take drugs to manage her gifts while Harper had lost her sister because of her desire to succeed, her need to control, and her inability to forgive. When they finished with their meeting, maybe they could fly together and once again find the freedom they had been missing.

The courtyard was empty except for the graceful trees and a blue picnic table that gave the yard a feel of an overgrown and under-utilized park. Gliding downward, Harper swung to the right and landed between a small patch of trees. Several offices' windows looked out into the courtyard, but no one seemed to be watching.

Starling dropped to the ground at her side. Close to their left was the main door. Behind the door's glass a skinny, alabaster colored man talked, his hands moving animatedly as he explained some unknown point to his co-worker. Careful to stay out of sight, Harper and Starling moved behind a shrub next to the entrance.

The door's hinges protested as the door opened and the blond man stepped out. "He can't just expect us to follow along. This is bullshit."

"Well you know how it is. Politics," his co-worker answered.

The two continued talking about a shared wrong, but Harper paid them no attention; instead she concentrated on the door. As soon as the men turned toward the blue picnic table, using the shrub for as much cover as she could, Harper rushed toward the door, catching it with her webbed foot just before it closed. She opened the door and waited for Starling to step inside before their one chance slammed shut.

Inside the door, they shifted back into their naked human forms. Harper tried to divert her eyes for Starling, looking anywhere but at the young woman.

"What are we going to do now?" Starling whispered. "We can't go meet the doctor naked."

Down the sterile white hallway was a door marked *Utility Closet*. There had to be something inside they could use. "Follow me."

Her heart thundered in her ears as they walked down the narrow hall. The familiar scent of antiseptics and the unmistakable bitter aroma of medications filled the air. In most ways, the place was just like Merckson, the same bitter scent, the same sterile laboratory environment, but something was different and Harper couldn't quite put her finger on what was wrong.

Opening the door to the closet, they slipped inside before anyone could see them. The closet was filled with mops and buckets, and against the far wall was a shelf filled with toilet paper, window cleaners, and waxes. Above the supplies and to the left sat a stack of dark blue coveralls. They would have to work.

Harper grabbed the coveralls and handed a set to Starling. "Here, take this and put it on." She slipped a pair over her bare flesh. The harsh fabric rubbed against her chilled skin, but it was better than nothing. Glancing over at Starling she bit back a nervous laugh—the pantsuit was about ten sizes too big for the young woman and hung on her like an old whale's skin.

"Laugh it up. You look just as stupid as I do," Starling retorted.

"I don't doubt it, but at least I don't think we're going to draw as much attention as if we were naked."

The young woman's delicate smile reappeared for a split second.

Harper opened the door and stepped out into the silent hall. Stepping around a corner, the hallway was lined with offices. Farther down, and behind bulletproof windows, lab coat wearing scientists bustled around a laboratory.

To her left was an office with the brass placard that read "Dr. Eliot McDougal, Pharm.D., M.S."

She knocked gently on the door, praying he wasn't one of the men standing in the laboratory at the end of the hall.

There was a click as the door opened and they were met by a bald man in a white lab coat. The coat was stretched tight over his stomach as the buttons struggled to stay closed. He wore black oversized glasses that made his eyes appear enlarged, giving him the look of a squashed bug. "Dr. Cygnini? Ms. Jackson?" he asked, recognizing them from their attempt at admittance. "What are you doing in here? I told them not to let you in."

"Dr. McDougal, it's nice to finally meet you," Harper said, as she and Starling slipped past him and into his office. "I've heard such wonderful things about you and your company. I'm sorry we had to meet like this, but you know how it is when you really need something." Her awkward laugh fell flat.

The small office was filled with empty soda cans and wrappers. On the wall, next to his computer, was a fading movie poster for *Lara Croft, Tomb Raider*. The only thing missing was a stack of Dungeons and Dragons cards and the man could have been a teenager right in the midst of his awkward high school years.

He blinked over and over as if he struggled to believe what he saw. "How did you get in here?"

"We have our ways. You can't stop determined women," she said, trying to play off their mysterious appearance into his office.

"I suppose, but I can see I'm going to have to learn more about women and our security," he said, almost in a socially awkward way, as if she was the first person he had talked to in days.

Harper couldn't control the smile that overtook her lips. This was going to be easier than she had anticipated. All she would need would be a little nymph wiles and he would be under her spell.

"So if you are so determined, you must really be desperate for a job. What kind of job are you looking for? Most of the time our HR department handles this kind of stuff."

Her smile widened. "Oh, I know and I appreciate your seeing us like this. I know how busy you must be with your new medications, I'm sure that is why you couldn't let us in." She turned her smile into the picture of innocence. "Aren't you working on a new breast cancer drug?"

His eyes tightened into a suspicious squint. "How do you know about Tribextra? That was supposed to be under wraps until next month, after the clinical trials."

"It seems to be working well on your test subjects. I heard one woman's cancer was cured within two months of starting your new drug regimen."

"Yes." The suspicious look on his face disappeared and was replaced by a look of pride. "It only took six weeks. The tumor's margins saw significant reduction. Tribextra will be touted as the new go-to medication in breast cancer treatment."

"Does it show any indication for use in other types of cancers?"

"We are looking into it, but the drug works at a nanoscale."

"So you are attacking the individual cancer cells versus the entire body?"

"Exactly," he said, his proud smile growing.

"You really enjoy helping others, don't you?" Harper wrapped her arm over Starling's shoulder.

"I suppose." He sat down at his computer and motioned for them to take the two chairs wedged behind the other side of the desk.

"I have to admit I was hoping you could help us with something." She gave him a seductive smile, letting her energy radiate toward him.

His eyes sparkled and there was a new radiance to his ruddy cheeks as her energy wrapped around him like a candy coating of sex. His chair squeaked as he leaned across the desk. "What kind of help are you looking for?"

An empty candy bar wrapper crinkled as she picked it up and moved it across the desk so she could lean closer. "We are something special." She motioned toward Starling.

"Yes, you are," he said in a daze.

"Thank you." Her grin tightened. "You've helped *our kind* before, a woman named Carey … with a certain kind of drug … Something that didn't pass clinical trials. Do you know what I'm talking about?"

The sparkle in his eyes receded. "You're not here for that, are you? I can't help you …"

She tiptoed her fingers across the desk until her fingers stopped on the top of his hand. Energy seeped from her touch and into his damp flesh, strengthening her seductive bond. "So you do know what I'm talking about? The anti-psychotic you've been delivering to Starling's mother, Carey?"

"I stopped all contact with Carey over a year ago."

"So you haven't seen her at all in the last year?"

Dr. McDougal shook his head. "She's tried calling, but I've been … unavailable."

"Do you think it is possible we could get any more of that particular medication?"

"We started work on that drug over twenty years ago. Now, it's all gone." The skin of his hand warmed and his body tensed under her touch.

"Why are you lying to me, Eliot?" She let her voice drip with sweetness.

"I gave her enough to last for five years, if she rationed it to her daughter." He glanced at Starling, like he was finally putting a face to a name.

Starling's lips were puckered as if she was trying to hold back from speaking.

"Eliot," Harper continued, rubbing her finger down the length of his index finger. "This is Starling Jackson, Carey's daughter. Can you look at her and tell her there is no more of the drug? That she will no longer get the *help* she so desperately needs? Are you really so crass?"

There was a flash of pain in his muddy brown eyes as his gaze slipped between her and Starling. "Even if there were more of GX 149, there's no way I could get my hands on it. They are keeping it under lock and key."

"Is there any way you could make more?"

Dr. McDougal sat back, pulling his hand from hers. "You know, as a pharmacologist, that is completely impossible. GX 149 didn't pass clinical testing and there is no way I can bring it back into the lab for personal use. That project is done."

"I also know if you can find another marketable use for the drug, or if you think you can tweak it to be effective without the side effects that failed it during clinical trials, that you can bring this drug back from the dead."

"You don't think I've already thought of that?" Dr. McDougal rebuked. "Don't you think we have had teams of people trying to figure out other ways to alter GX 149? It simply can't be done."

"Maybe you and I could work together to make this happen. I could quit Merckson and we could spend every day together." She was grasping at straws ... "Do you think I could see the information on the drug?"

Dr. McDougal's smile weakened and she could feel her energy slow as it struggled to leave her. "You know as well as I do we can't share information. I like you." He leaned forward. "But there's just no way that I can give you what you're asking."

Starling stiffened in her seat. "Eliot?" she asked tentatively. "I know that you have your job to think of, I do. But I can't be without my medicine. I'm so scared."

Dr. McDougal's gaze dropped down to his desk.

"I'm scared the next time, if I go into my own mind, I may not come back." Her fingers shook violently in her lap. "Do you know what it's like to be constantly in contact with spirits—most of which you don't want? I only want to talk to my mother ... my dead mother ... This medication ... I think your medication is the reason she's dead."

The young woman hurt and her pain and fear made Harper's heart pang with sympathy. "Starling, it's okay. If he can't help us ... we can find another way. You don't have to talk about this. You don't have to do this to yourself."

"I want him to know," Starling said. "I want him to know how important this medication is to me. He needs to know GX 149 is the only way I will be able to function … If I can function then I can find whoever killed my mother." She turned to Dr. McDougal. "I need to find her killer."

"If you can talk to the dead … " Dr. McDougal started. "Then why haven't you asked your mother who killed her?"

"I can ask, but I don't have great enough control over my ability yet. I can barely get out of my bed in the morning … And now … since my mother's death, the only reason I have left to wake up, is to find whoever killed my mother and get my revenge."

Starling's agony shook Harper to her core. She was just like Harper—filled with the anguish of loss and the passion for some type of vengeance.

"Eliot, please. If there is anything you can do to help her … us … please."

He stared down at his hands for a second and then looked up. "There's nothing—"

"Eliot, did you know my sister?" Harper interrupted his refusal. "Did you know Jenna Cygnini?"

His buggy eyes widened, making them look as though they barely fit under his bottle-thick lenses. "I know your sister … How is she?" Subtle warmth crept into his voice.

All of a sudden the razor and the shaving kit in Jenna's bathroom came to mind—was it possible that this man, this lab coat wearing, nerdy man, had left the shaving kit behind?

"She's not good." Harper baited the trap.

"What? What happened to her? Her phone's been off. I've been leaving messages," he said, the words suddenly fighting to get out.

"When's the last time you saw Jenna?" Harper asked.

"I went to her house three weeks ago, but no one was home."

"Let me get this right—you hadn't seen Carey in a year, but you just went to see my sister?"

As she asked the question, Dr. McDougal's shoulder's rose and he cowered slightly. "Yes."

"What happened between you and Carey?"

Dr. McDougal's shoulder rose higher so none of his neck was exposed. "She found out your sister and I were trying to do something, something she didn't like. Carey wanted us to stop. So Jenna stopped telling her about me. I quit delivering to Carey and only had contact with Jenna."

"When was the last time you saw Jenna?" Starling pressed.

He seemed to think for a moment. "It was six weeks ago, but I normally try to see her at least every three weeks. We've been having a bit of a rough patch."

"Are you dating?" Harper asked in a soft, caring voice.

"We are. At least I think we are, but like I said she hasn't been taking my calls. I knew she was angry with me, but I've been trying to explain to her how sorry I am."

"The last time I saw her I told her I couldn't get GX 149. She wasn't happy that I had come empty-handed." He balled his hands. "I thought she really loved me—that she wanted to be with me for something more than the drugs. But I guess I was wrong. I don't know why she was so upset—she had been tucking the drugs away for a while now. Between her house and the safe deposit box there should have been a big enough supply to do what she was trying to do."

"There's a safe deposit box?"

"So far as I know."

"How big is this supply? How long can we help Starling?"

"There was a five year supply for Starling and another five year supply to help with our experiment. There should have been plenty of drugs for her to get everything she wanted."

"What experiment are you talking about?"

"You know. She wanted a baby … "

Her gasp echoed through the room. She should have known. She should have known how desperate her sister had been to have a baby—that this all went back to her sister's desire for children. It was the same desperate desire that had gotten her killed.

Harper tried to get her thoughts in order, but sadness and regret filled the pit in her heart and overflowed into her tired mind. Words refused to form on her lips.

"What do you mean?" Starling reached over and sat her warm hand atop Harper's, comforting her. "Why would GX 149 help a nymph get pregnant?"

"One of the side effects of the drug is that it aids in women's fertility. With most of these types of medication, they cause ovarian damage and reduce fertility. However, with GX 149, it actually strengthens the ovaries and increases the quality and quantities of the ovum." A weak smile played on his face as he seemed to take pride in the drug. "In other words, the women who take GX 149 get more, higher quality, eggs. In the case of Jenna, she was hoping it would be enough to get her pregnant."

"But it didn't work?" Harper said, trying to center herself back in reality.

"You don't know anything about your sister, do you? I know you two aren't close, but I didn't know you were so distant." His proud smile disappeared.

"I know." Her fingers ached as she loosened her grip on the chair's armrests. "It's something I will regret for the rest of time. I should have never left her alone."

"She loves you, Harper. She talks about you all the time—especially when she went through the miscarriage."

"What ... miscarriage?" Her sorrow showered every nerve in her body with excruciating pain. Why hadn't Jenna told her? Why hadn't she called? Tears filled Harper's eyes.

"It was a couple of months ago. She and I ... we were ... it was a girl. She was going to name her Harper—after you."

She couldn't keep the tears from slipping down her cheeks. Just when she thought she could feel no greater pain than her sister's loss the pain was amplified.

"I love your sister, but as soon as I told her I loved her, she stopped talking to me. Then she disappeared. I just don't understand it."

Harper's tears blurred her vision, and she tried to choke back the sounds of her crying. She needed to be stronger than this. "It … was … the curse."

"What curse?" Dr. McDougal looked to Starling for answers.

"Nymphs can't love. If they fall in love, the man they choose is fated to die. The bastard Zeus placed the curse on our kind forever ago," Starling answered.

"Is that why she chose me? Was I unlovable?" Dr. McDougal asked, his voice pensive.

Harper dabbed at her eyes. "She left because you were loveable—when we really love someone we have to leave. It's the only way we can keep them safe. It's our only choice."

"Where is Jenna? Is that why she isn't here? Because she loves me?"

"No," Harper answered, a fresh tear upon her cheek. "She isn't here because … because she's dead."

"What? Are you serious? She's … she's … dead?" The word "dead" came out as a whisper.

"Yes, and I will be soon, if you don't help me. I need more GX 149. Please," Starling begged.

Dr. McDougal gave a slow, dazed nod. "The drugs are gone, but I'll see what I can do. Where are you staying?"

"At the Bellagio, in the penthouse," Starling answered.

Harper tried to control her emotions, but it was a losing battle. "Why don't you meet us in the Business Center lobby? Two hours. Please. Bring the paperwork … Bring anything that will help."

Chapter Twenty

The bodyguard walked into the penthouse suite carrying an aluminum briefcase shackled to his wrist. "Was everything okay while I was gone, sir?"

Kodie followed him in and made his way across the room.

"Everything is fine, Jeffries." Mr. Blackwater, the gaming commissioner, dropped his hands to the armrests of the gold embossed chair. "Going back to what we were talking about, Chance, do you understand what I'm asking of you?"

"Let me get this right. You want to catch Nate cheating by setting me up as bait?"

Mr. Blackwater gave a stoic nod. "Exactly."

"How do you think he's cheating?"

"We think he's using collusion."

Chance's skin prickled with the nastiness of the word. For a second, his mind went to the night Kodie had taken the loan. He'd been getting pretty lucky cards. He'd played them well, but at the time Chance had blamed the losing on Kodie's inability to control his emotions and his tells. Yet, thinking back, he remembered the other man, Vice, at Kodie and Nate's table that night. He'd been betting loose, throwing around big bets, making the other players think he had the cards, but when it came to the river, the last card, several times he folded. At the time, Chance had thought the man was just a shitty poker player, but maybe he'd gotten it all wrong. Maybe the man was working with Nate. Maybe he'd been signaling the cards.

"How many players do you think Nate's using?"

"Going back in our video archives, we've seen Nate and another man, Vice, together at the Bellagio high-stakes several times. Each time Nate or Vice has walked out a winner."

Kodie turned away from the window, his face was pale. "How could I miss it, Chance? How could I have been so stupid?"

"Don't beat yourself up, Kodie. I missed it too."

"Goddamn him … We gotta do something. We can't let him get away with this bullshit."

He couldn't blame Kodie for his anger. He'd been conned and they would have to get their revenge, but maybe they could get something else at the same time. Chance couldn't draw his eyes away from the bodyguard's briefcase as the bodyguard passed him and walked into the kitchen. He laid the square box on the expensive looking black marble countertop and dropped his hands onto the metal. With one simple "yes," what lay inside could be Chance's.

"How much are you going to pay us to help take Nate down?"

"I'll give you everything that is in that case." Mr. Blackwater pointed at the case still shackled to the bodyguard's wrist. "And more … . Depending on your level of *cooperation*." Mr. Blackwater leaned forward and offered his hand. "Do we have a deal?"

The cheater, Nate, needed to be stopped, but if Chance said yes to the gaming commissioner it would mean his reputation would come into question with the other players. He might as well be making a deal with the devil.

"What if I say no?" Chance squirmed in the straight-backed chair as if the golden fabric was responsible for the uncomfortable situation in which he found himself.

Mr. Blackwater's lips pulled into a dangerous smile. "If you choose to not work with us, then I shall assume you're going to play against us."

Going against the gaming commissioner was the last thing Chance wanted to do, but he didn't want to be implicated in any of their plans. "I've worked my entire career to develop a reputation of being fair and a man of honor—I can't just throw it all away."

Kodie stepped beside him. "Chance is right, Mr. Blackwater. Nate is one helluva bastard, but there's a lot riding on tonight's game. And what if Nate doesn't cheat tonight? We still got debts that need to be paid. We can't be involved in another deal where we could end up owing anyone anything. We ... " He shot a look over at Chance. "I mean *I*, learned my lesson."

"You have, have you?" A cynical laugh rippled from Blackwater.

"Absolutely. I'm not going to put Chance in any more danger. We just need to pay back Three-Eyed Nate and then we'll be done with this mess."

"You know about our history in Vegas don't you, Kodie?" Mr. Blackwater looked like a snake in the way his lips peeled back from his teeth.

"You aren't threatening us, are you, Mr. Blackwater?" Chance tried to act cool.

"Absolutely not. I'm merely asking if you men know Las Vegas started as a mafia town." Mr. Blackwater's dangerous smile grew wider. "No one in this place went against the bosses. More importantly, no one took what didn't belong to them—there are many graves in the desert filled with the bones of those who tried."

"Don't you have another way to take Nate down?"

"There are other ways we can handle this situation, but we are hoping to not use such antiquated practices in taking down those we deem "less than ideal" for our business. We'd rather use this instance to our advantage."

By using *him*. "We haven't acted in a way that is *less than ideal*."

"Not yet, but if you aren't willing to help us, I'm sure we can find something in your past we don't like ... something we could use to show how you and Kodie are going to go against the bosses." Mr. Blackwater straightened his black jacket and the sudden movement made Chance's heart pound. The man meant business.

The bodyguard thumped his fingers on the metal briefcase. "I think I saw an area out in the desert … a perfect place where a grave … or two, would never be found."

"You wouldn't go against your best interests, would you?" Mr. Blackwater stood up and pulled his sleeves down, covering the wrists of his white dress shirt.

"Let me think about it." Chance stood up and faced the man head-on.

"I don't understand what there is to think about." Mr. Blackwater motioned to his bodyguard and the briefcase. "I trust you will make the right choice."

"You can't just force this on us," Chance said, pointing at the bodyguard and the gilded threat.

"We're not forcing anything," Mr. Blackwater answered, with a calmness that came to men in power. "We're only trying to impress upon you how important your role in this game is going to be."

"*If* I play along."

Mr. Blackwater smiled and walked toward the door, the case-wielding bodyguard close at his heels. "I'm sure you will do what you know is right."

The door clicked shut behind them, leaving confusion in their wake.

"Shit." Kodie turned and walked back to his spot at the window. "Shit. Shit."

What was Chance going to do? If things didn't go as they hoped, they would still have to pay back the debts owed. In the winner-take-all tournament there was only one winner, and only one way he could come up with the money to pay back Three-Eyed Nate. They had to win. However, if they took Nate and Vice down, Kodie's debt would no longer be an issue.

Walking away from a debt owed wasn't that simple. Yeah, it would have been great to forget about the money owed, but if the word spread Chance had been involved in taking Nate and Vice down all hell would break loose. Some players would love that he took down a cheater, but they would never forget he had worked with the authorities. Even if they thanked him to his face, the other big name players would be calling him a narc behind his back.

Kodie faced out toward the strip. "Blackwater is an idiot if he thinks he is going to get away with this. There is no way his plan is going to work."

Chance couldn't disagree—Blackwater's plan was never going to work, but the man was far from being an idiot. What Blackwater wanted from them was outside of the realm of acceptability, but they only had one choice—they had to play the gaming commissioner's game or they would have to get out of Vegas—permanently.

If he was going to continue being one of the best poker players in the world, he couldn't do it anywhere but in Vegas. Yet, the more he thought, the more he couldn't discount the idea of leaving Vegas forever—a part of him was growing weary of this way of life. Yes, he loved to travel. To play poker. To win. However, there was another part of him that seemed to come alive when he was around Harper. He loved being with her. Listening to her talk. She hated the idea of his drifter ways, but did he love her enough to give it all up?

He faced a difficult choice—continue on the road he'd been traveling for so long and do what the commissioner asked, or give up on this reclusive life and put his heart on the line.

"What are we gonna do, Chance?" Kodie leaned his head against the plate glass window. "We're damned if we do and we're more than damned if we don't."

"Kodie, we're going to play the game … but we may just have to play by our own rules."

Chance's phone buzzed in his breast pocket, pulling his attention away from the mess. Grabbing the phone, he stared down at the most beautiful named he'd ever read—Harper.

"Hi," he answered, pressing the phone to his ear. "How'd it go?"

"I think we got somewhere with Dr. McDougal. He's going to meet us in two hours. He said he would bring all the information he could get his hands on." There was an edge of excitement in Harper's voice, but beneath the thin layer there was something else.

"What's wrong, sweetheart?"

"I got a call."

"From?"

Kodie turned from the window and took a few steps toward him, as if he wanted to hear what Harper was saying.

"Ariadne Papadakis, the leader of the sisterhood of Epione. She said she has a man tailing Starling and me."

"What? Why would the sisterhood have someone tailing you?"

"They think we could be in danger. Jenna's house was broken into right after we left."

"Did they take anything?"

There was a pause on the other end of the phone. "Ariadne said they only saw a woman."

"Do they know who the woman was?"

"No. Ariadne just said it was a mousy woman. They seem to think she is connected somehow to Carey's death—and now, whoever she is, she may be targeting us."

"Why?"

"I have a feeling it has something to do with Carey's ability to have a child … " She paused for a long moment, making him wonder if she had wanted a baby.

"You don't want a child, do you?"

"No," Harper said, but there was sadness in her voice. "But I never thought I had a choice. Until after you and I made love. I thought maybe with Carey getting pregnant, I could too."

"And you were excited?"

"I guess. But I never really thought about having a child before. I think I was more excited to have the option. But it was stupid to even think about. If Ariadne is right and the drugs are the reason Carey got pregnant, than there is no way I could be." Harper paused on the other end of the phone line. "So don't worry, you won't be having any more children."

He hadn't even thought of the possibility of a pregnancy. "I'm sorry, Harper."

"Don't be sorry. I could have had a child a hundred years ago, but it didn't fit in my life."

That was one sentiment Chance could understand. Only a week ago, he had felt the same way. But since adding Starling to his life there was no way he would go back to the way things had been. If anything he looked forward to the future more than he ever had before.

"What about now?" Chance paused. "Do you think you'd want a child around now? Maybe a child like Starling?"

"What do you mean, Chance?"

What did he mean? Harper couldn't be in his life. She had her own in Seattle. "Nothing. Never mind. What else did Ariadne tell you?"

"Ariadne seemed concerned with the drugs getting in the wrong hands. If Starling, her drug, or the formula ends up in the wrong hands, she thinks we may have more incidents like what the ranchers tried to do with Jenna. And who knows what else supernaturals would do if they had a way to guarantee a pregnancy—she couldn't guarantee that Starling would be safe."

He had a hard time understanding her words. It was as if they were coming through water. He just couldn't believe someone out there wanted to hurt his daughter just so they could have the chance to have a child of their own.

Harper continued, unaware of how her words swam into his overworked mind. "So many types of supernaturals can't get pregnant—they are desperate. And may the gods help us if we have a population boom of someone or something that has no business breeding."

"If I find out who did this ... Who killed Carey ... Who wants to hurt Starling ... Or you ... " Anger seeped through him like a liquid flame. "Getting pregnant will be the last thing they'll have to worry about. They won't live long enough."

"There's something else."

What could possibly be worse than hearing there were people out there who would be trying to hurt the only two women in the world he cared about? "Are you kidding me?"

"Ariadne told me Jenna had been using the drugs as well. She'd gotten pregnant. And then ... well, she lost the baby."

The anger, that had only seconds before overwhelmed him, suddenly turned to a sickening mix of rage, confusion, and sadness. "Oh my God, Harper. I'm so sorry."

There was a siren somewhere in the background on Harper's end of the line. "It's okay."

She needed his help. She needed him to protect her. She couldn't be alone. Not now. Not when she was so exposed. So vulnerable. "Harper, come back to the penthouse. Please."

"I just wish I would have known. I missed so much. If only I could have been there for Jenna."

"Honey, you didn't do anything wrong. Your sister died because of her choices and the people she ran with. You couldn't have changed things for her." He tried to comfort her, but even as he spoke, he knew what he was saying wasn't really the truth. Maybe if Harper had been more involved in Jenna's life she could have made a difference—just as he could have made a difference in Carey's. Maybe he could have stopped her from dying—from getting wrapped up in a drug trade and conspiracy in which she had no business being involved.

"Maybe you're right, maybe I couldn't have changed anything, but I could have tried."

"You're right, but there's no use in going over things that we can't change. We did the best we could. And now the best thing we can do is keep you and Starling safe and get the hell out of Las Vegas. Maybe we just need to run away and find a place where we can all be safe."

"No more running." She paused. "Just today I told Starling there are times when we need to walk away and times when we need to fight. I think this is one of those times we need to fight. Starling needs the medication and you have a tournament to win."

He tried to hold back the snort, but the sound escaped. "Right. *Win* the tournament."

"What's that supposed to mean?"

"Nothing," he lied. There was a tournament, yes, but he was only a pawn and not a player. "Just come back. I need to know you are okay. I need you in my arms."

Chapter Twenty-One

Maybe if Harper just went back to Seattle she could put this all behind her, but she'd made a promise she intended to keep. There was no way to turn back now and leave Starling without the help she needed; and she couldn't leave Chance … not when he needed her the most.

"Chance, what time do you have to sign in at the game?" Harper asked, trying to make the worried expression on his face disappear.

He looked up at her. "Hmm. What did you say?"

"What time do you need to go down to Bobby's Room for the tournament?"

"Not for another two hours. Then the gaming commissioner will go over the table stakes and the rules of the game."

Kodie and Starling huddled together at the table. "Why don't Starling and I run downstairs, and get everything in order? I don't think the commissioner will mind if I sign you in for the game. I would venture a guess he is willing to make a few allowances for you today."

"I can do it, really," Chance said, his voice tired.

"Let me just take care of it," Kodie repeated.

Getting up, Chance walked over to his rucksack and pulled out his checkbook. Opening up the little leather book, he lifted a pen and wrote out a check. "Here's my buy-in. Please make sure it gets into the right hands."

"Got it, boss," Kodie said, taking the check and stuffing it into his pocket.

"I'm hungry," Starling said, interrupting the conversation.

"And I'll get the little miss something to eat." Kodie nodded as he looked to Starling. "Can't have you starving on us. We're gonna need you to cheer for your old man tonight," he said, giving Starling's hand a light pat. "He's gonna need a lot of support."

Harper couldn't make sense of what the men eluded to. What had the gaming commissioner and Chance talked about? Ever since she and Starling had returned to the room on the thirty-fifth floor, there had been a stillness that somehow reminded Harper of Jenna's funeral. It was like she was standing at the head of the casket, waiting for people to pass by and leave her with hollow condolences. Chance couldn't even look her in the eyes. It didn't matter whether it was out of fear or shame, Harper couldn't go through another day where the people she knew and cared about couldn't stand to face her.

Kodie and Starling walked to the door, but Kodie turned back. "Why don't you get some rest, Chance? You know what I always say: *If your mind's a mess so is your game.*"

"I'm going to go too. I have to meet Dr. McDougal." Harper glanced down at her watch. She had plenty of time, but she couldn't stand being in the room any longer. "You should take a nap."

"Do you need me to go with you, Harper?" Kodie asked as he and Starling moved toward the door.

"No. I got this. It may be better if it is just me who goes to see him. I don't want to draw any attention."

Harper stood up to follow Kodie and Starling.

"Wait," Chance said, sticking out his hand for her to take it. "Don't go. Not yet. Please."

The way he pleaded made Harper stop and sit back down into the golden chair at Chance's side. How had Chance become a broken man in just a matter of hours?

From the first time Harper had seen him sitting behind the poker table in Worley, he had been happy, easy-going, and filled with a passion Harper now realized she secretly envied. It was his passion that had first infuriated her—a love for travel and poker she hadn't fully understood—but now, seeing how it affected him, it was easy to see it was his calling. Playing the game was like breathing—it was necessary.

It was a passion she had never had in her life—not even in her work. Yes, she'd been dedicated and selfless in getting the next drug out to consumers, getting the next safe and effective drug developed, or the next drug from concept to application—but her work wasn't driven by passion. No. It was driven by the need to run and hide from her mistakes and the loneliness of her life.

If being around Chance, Kodie, and Starling had taught her anything, it was that going back to her old way of life was going to be hard. Unfortunately, it was something she was going to have to do. The level of passion that Chance held for the game was something he would never be able to replicate. More to the point, he would never be able to love her as much as he loved the game. And standing second to a deck of cards and the click of poker chips was not something Harper was willing to accept—no matter how much she cared about the disheveled cowboy.

"We'll see you guys at tonight's game," Kodie said, almost as if it was more of a command than a hope or request. The door clicked shut.

"Are you really thinking about not going to tonight's game?"

Chance's fingers dug into the finely sewn edges of the chair. "I have to go. You heard Kodie."

"What did the gaming commissioner want?"

His finger's drove deeper into the fabric, so deep Harper wondered how much the chair could withstand, how much it could endure before it would tear under the pressure.

Chance slid from the chair, down to his knees in front of her. "Let's not talk about this anymore. I just need a break." He took her hands and interlaced his fingers with hers. "Like I told you on the phone, I just want you in my arms. I need to feel you again."

She didn't know how to react. He wanted her, but did she want *this*? She peered down at the rounded edges of his nails and the tanned skin on the back of his hand. His hands were just like him—tender and strong, giving and needing.

If they did this, if she let herself be swept away into his arms, it would have to be the last time. She couldn't risk everything that would be at stake—her heart, his future, and his life. And even if they found a way around the curse, she couldn't ask him to give up poker, and if she fell for this man, someone was going to have to compromise for things to work out. Either she would have to give up her job and the comfort of her routine in Seattle, or he would have to give up his drifter lifestyle.

Both she and Chance were so defined by their careers. It was hard for her to imagine a life without her job. For a fleeting moment, her mind wandered to the thoughts of what life would be like following Chance around the country, from one dive bar to the next while he banked on the fact that his hereditary advantage would keep him playing for at least one more night. There was just too much risk.

"Chance, we can't do this … We can't be together like this … "

"Why can't we have this moment?" He looked up at her and there was a deep rolling sadness in his gaze. He must have known just as well as she that there was nothing beyond this last night together. As soon as she got the formula from Dr. McDougal, and as soon as Chance finished the tournament and they returned to Idaho, they would have to go their separate ways. The only time they might ever see each other again would be when and *if* she could make a drug that could help Starling—and that was a long shot.

"We made a promise … We agreed the other night was going to be the only time. It's too dangerous. And you know it, Chance."

He dropped his hands down to her knees. The heat of his touch sank into her skin, making some of the delicate snowflakes of her resolve melt away.

"Why do you always have to look at the negative? Why can't you just live for the moment? Live for this second. Right here. Right now."

"That's what Jenna did. And look where she ended up. I can't handle losing another person in my life. It's better to walk away now than to let anything happen." She tried to be angry, she tried to force her body to stand up and run away from his wanting touch, but her body refused.

"You don't have to be afraid to love."

"Yes, I do, Chance." She looked down to their entwined fingers. "There's nothing I fear more."

"Then tell yourself you don't love me."

"What about the curse Chance? Even if there is the possibility of you getting hurt it can't be worth loving me. You have a daughter to think about."

"I love Starling. She's a nymph. I'm in danger, but I'm not going to stop loving her—or you. We are going to just deal with the future one day at a time. We aren't immortal and death may come to me, but at least we can love each other until that day. And if I'm taken, I will love you from the heavens."

It was too late to keep from loving him, but he still couldn't know how badly she wanted to give him her heart.

He wrapped his hands around hers and pressed them together over his heart. "If you really don't care about me, tell me ... Tell me that and I will walk away. I will go downstairs, go to my game, and never look back. I won't bother you again. Or you can give me this moment, you can make love to me and let go of everything that is holding you back. We can make this work. We can escape, at least for a moment, into each other. Please. Let me love—"

"Stop. Chance. Just stop." Her heart ached. She wanted to fall down to her knees, feel the moist pleasure of his kiss, but it just couldn't be. They were too different. Too far apart. It was too far into the unknown, too dangerous.

"If that's the way you feel, just tell me … Tell me you don't care … that you don't love me … Let me put a stop to the confusing mess I'm feeling. I'll just take Starling and she and I can go back to my old life. Starling will be okay."

It would be so much easier for everyone involved. Harper couldn't risk everyone's safety and the security and comfort of the known to take a chance on something that would probably never work … He was a broken man and the only way she could fix things for him was to leave. "Chance." She trembled as she rose to her feet. "I don't love you."

Chapter Twenty-Two

The business lounge was filled with people in black. Black suits, black dresses, and black expressions. It seemed unlikely the rest of them had just lied and told the most important person in their life they didn't love them—that they didn't want a future, when in fact it was the one thing they wanted above anything else. But there were times when even a demigod had to be selfless. Life wasn't a fairy tale. Life was life, hard, filled with anger, lies, deception, and death. If Harper could stop just one person she loved from dying by keeping away, then that was what had to be done—she'd already lost her sister, she couldn't lose another person she loved.

The chair dug into the back of Harper's legs as if even it wanted her to move along, like it knew she would only bring death to those around her. Shifting to ease the pressure, she glanced down at her watch.

Dr. McDougal was late. She should have never trusted him to come through on his word. He had nothing to gain in their agreement. Her only hope was that her seduction and appealing to his softer side had paid off—if not, hell would have no greater fury.

If he didn't come, they would be in the same situation—no answers, only a limited supply of drugs, and a bleak future for Starling. The only option the young woman would have would be to turn into her animal form. She would have to stay there until Harper could find something, anything, that would help Starling deal with the spirits which haunted her day and night, taunting and pressing her to communicate through words that were often best left unwritten and unanswered.

If Harper couldn't help her, Starling would have no future, no hope for a somewhat normal life. And once again, Harper would disappoint another person—just like she had let Jenna down. She couldn't make the same mistake again.

The edge of the seat cut deeper into her skin. Unable to stand the annoyance any longer, Harper stood up. To her right, down a dimly lit hall, was a women's restroom. One more time, Harper glanced around the business lounge, but Dr. McDougal wasn't to be seen. She couldn't help feeling this was like watching a pot of water and waiting for it to boil. She walked to the restroom—if this worked like the rest of her life, he would show up while she was away.

The anteroom of the restroom matched the rest of the Bellagio with its gold and suede-covered chairs that were beautiful, but ill-suited for comfort. Passing through the empty room, she made her way to the row of gold sinks with matching gold faucets. Dropping her purse on the counter next to the sink, she stared up at her reflection in the mirror. The week had been drawing on her like a ravenous suckling babe, leaving only a skeletal woman with deep bags beneath her once light-filled eyes.

It would soon be all over. In a few days, she would be back in Seattle, but no matter how hard she tried, she couldn't convince herself that life would return to normal. Yes, she would be home, but too much had changed in the last week. Life would never be the same. She no longer had family. And she'd constantly be barraged with thoughts of what might have been with Chance had she made a different choice.

Digging through her purse, she found her lipstick and pressed the waxy tip to her lips, covering them with the fake color. She dabbed her lips on a tissue, and once again stared at her reflection. She couldn't draw her eyes away from the red hues. The color was a counterfeit in the way it promised of life and beauty, but instead covered the dull prospect that was she, and her future. If she went back to Seattle, her job would be just like the fake color—it would only be there for the sake of appearances, but beneath it all would be the pale nothingness that came with being empty and alone.

Unable to bear her reflection any longer, Harper turned away just as a man with fear-filled eyes staggered into the bathroom.

"Harper," Dr. McDougal's strangled voice echoed through the cavernous space. "Run. Don't give her your sister's keys."

"What keys?"

Dr. McDougal dropped to the floor, and a manila envelope fell out of his jacket. A needle protruded from his neck.

Harper moved to run, but there was nowhere to go. She was trapped.

Standing behind the body was a small beak-nosed woman. The woman smiled, reminding Harper of a bird in the way woman's beady eyes skimmed over the room before settling upon her like she was the next prey to scavenge.

"Harper, I've been looking for you." The woman stepped forward and picked up the manila envelope from the floor with a confused frown. Shrugging indifferently, she stuffed the envelope into her purse.

Dr. McDougal twitched on the floor as the convulsions of death rippled through his body.

"Who are you?"

The woman smiled; her small teeth only lacked dripping blood to make her appear more frightening. "Don't you remember me? I'm offended."

Then it struck her—the beak-nosed woman was the woman from Jenna's funeral. She'd spent so much time thinking about Carey and Chance that she'd almost completely forgotten about the chief medical examiner. "What are you doing here, Dr. Redbird?" Harper tried not to stare as Dr. McDougal's legs bounced around the floor like fish out of water.

"You have something I want."

What was the woman talking about? The only thing she had was her job and a little bit of money, neither of which the doctor could have wanted. "I don't have anything to give you."

"That's where you're wrong." Dr. Redbird stepped over Dr. McDougal's quivering body, coming much too close to Harper. She scanned the room for anything she could use to defend herself, but Harper found nothing.

The doctor reached down into her purse and extracted another needle filled with some type of clear fluid. "If you do what I ask, I won't have to kill you. If you refuse, you will end up just like this idiot." She jabbed the body with the tip of her red, alligator skin high heel. "I tried to tell him, but he wanted to play hardball, to lie and say he didn't know what I was talking about ... You don't want to end up like him, do you?"

Harper shook her head. She had no idea what Dr. Redbird was talking about and she wasn't sure that she wanted to find out.

"Are you going to help me?" There was a strange, crazed look in Dr. Redbird's eyes. Harper took a step toward the door, but Dr. Redbird stepped in her way. "There's no escape. You will do as I wish or you will die, just like Carey."

"What? You killed her?" Her words were less of a question and more of an accusation. She thought of how Jenna had tried to warn her by having Starling write the word "red." Had Jenna been telling her to watch for Dr. *Red*bird?

She was answered with the tight-lipped smile of the crazed woman. "If she would have just given me the drugs, none of this would have ever happened. But no ... Her damned daughter was more important. Just give me the GX 149 and I'll leave you with your life."

With Dr. McDougal dead, there would be no more drugs, only the little bit which she still had to ration out to Starling. If she gave Dr. Redbird what little they had left, there would be nothing.

Starling would be lost. Unless the manila envelope Dr. McDougal had dropped carried the formula to GX 149 ...

Harper needed to get the envelope—it was the only hope she had left to help Starling.

"What do you want with the drugs?" Harper asked, trying not to stare at the woman's purse.

"I don't think that's any of your business. All you need to worry about is giving me what I want."

"You can't kill me," Harper said, taking another step toward the door.

Dr. Redbird's cackle echoed through the stony bathroom. "That's where you're wrong." She lifted a thin strand of her mousy brown hair and twirled it in her fingers. "You may think you and your little shifter friends are immortal, but I know better. You, just like Carey, would be easy to dispatch."

Harper shrank back from the woman and brushed down her hair.

"Don't act shocked. Didn't you stop to think anything was amiss when none of your sister's *peculiarities* showed up in the autopsy report? Only someone like me, someone who knew the truth of the world and your kind, could have covered it so neatly. "

"I've never even read the autopsy report," she wheezed.

"I can't believe you didn't think more of my work than to not even read my eloquent report. I did a fabulous job of concealing the truth. I thought at least someone like you, someone who has spent her whole life dodging the secret and curse of her kind, could appreciate my efforts."

"Did you have something to do with ... with Jenna's death?" A stream of rage gurgled up from her depths at the mere thought.

The woman released another vile cackle. "Those men were stupid, but they were onto something. Why can't supernaturals like us have children? Why can't we have what most humans take for granted?"

Supernaturals like us, she'd said. But Harper knew Dr. Redbird was nothing like her—from the look of the woman, she was no nymph. And from the dead man at her feet, they couldn't have been more different. She would have never killed an innocent. Dr. McDougal had been a lab geek, but he'd never posed a threat. He hadn't deserved to die.

Harper glared at her.

"Don't look at me like that … Not all of us can be as lucky to be pretty and popular as you and your weak little sisterhood of nymphs. Some of us have to work for what we get in life. Some of us aren't blessed with popularity and seduction. You and your kind aren't anything but a bunch of stuck up little sluts."

"You don't know anything about me … or my kind."

"Oh really? Are you really going to try and tell me you haven't been fucking that pompous asshole, Chance Landon?"

The wind rushed from Harper's lungs.

Dr. Redbird's disgusting smile widened. "I bet you want to go running to him right now, don't you? You and your kind always need a man to rescue you … you sluts."

The anger that pulsed through Harper's veins seized her mind. "Fuck off. I don't give a shit if you kill me. You aren't getting anything, you bitch."

"The good thing about me and my kind is that we take what we want. We don't care what you feeble little things think. I'll get what I want one way or another."

"What are you?"

"I'm a Catharterian."

"A vulture-shifter?" Dr. Redbird, the humble civil servant who focused her life on working with the dead? Of course. The woman was a scavenger, feasting on the woes of others. If only Harper had been paying more attention, maybe she would have seen the woman for what she really was, but no, she had been too wrapped up in her affairs to take into account everything that had been going on around her.

Dr. Redbird scoffed. "Don't act like you are better than me. You're not. I'm the one holding the death juice, remember?" She lifted the needle and jiggled its contents. "You are going to give me the GX 149."

"No. I don't care if you kill me."

"Then I will kill your precious little halfling, Starling, and your dirty lover, Chance."

"You wouldn't hurt them."

Dr. Redbird's foot connected with Dr. McDougal's motionless body. "Wanna make a bet?"

Harper glanced down at Dr. McDougal's eyes. They stared out at nothingness. For a brief second, she wondered what it would be like to have no more pain, no more choices, and no more guilt. In a way, Dr. McDougal's lifeless body was enviable, all of his imperfections, every mistake he had made were now forgiven and forgotten. He was sinless.

If Harper gave up, if she let this vile, carrion-fed vulture win, she would die knowing she gave up—and would die a coward. Harper was many things: workaholic, control freak, bull-headed, but she'd never once thought of herself as a coward—and she wasn't about to start being one now, not when so many people depended on her, now when she could really make a difference.

She loved Starling. She loved Chance. Life would always be hard, but maybe she could make it a little easier for the people she loved. And right now, the best thing she could do for the both of them was play along with the crazed vulture.

"Fine. The drugs are yours."

"Good. I didn't want to have to take things this far. I'm glad you finally see the light. If only Carey could have listened and handed over the drugs. I would have never had to kill her."

Harper tried to quell the fear rising in her belly. A vulture couldn't be trusted. The insatiable greed for death and mayhem was their calling card. Death always followed in their wake.

"I've been watching you, Harper." The woman dropped the needle, the plastic cylinder resting on her black pants. "I see the way you fawn over Starling, like she is some little girl in need of saving. You need to know the truth. You need to know where she came from. What kind of woman her mother really was … All Carey cared about was herself and her drugs. The only good thing she ever did was die."

"She didn't deserve to die just because she wasn't willing to put her daughter in danger and give you the drugs. She was a great mom. She was willing to die to help the one she loved."

"Oh don't act like Carey Jackson was innocent. Really, I think I did you a favor in getting rid of that woman." The doctor shoved the needle down into her purse. "Now, if you aren't going to do what I tell you, then I will just go after Starling. That little bitch will give me everything I need."

Harper took in a deep breath. "I'll take you up to the penthouse. I only have a small amount of GX 149 left, but I'll give you everything I have."

Chapter Twenty-Three

The snapping sound of the cards mixed with the click of the plastic chips as the players sat down around the poker table. The familiar noises made Chance's skin tingle with excitement. When he was away for a few days it was easy to forget how much he loved this game, but sitting here, surrounded by the sounds of the tournament chips and the nervous chatter of his competitors, it all pulled him back in. This was the life he was meant to live. It was just too bad Harper couldn't see the value of his dreams.

She had said she didn't love him. Nothing had ever hurt him more … not his divorce … nothing. It had been ridiculous of him to assume what he had been feeling was going to work out. He'd been an idiot. He should've followed his gut when he'd first met her. A woman like her was never going to want to be with a drifter like him. She had proven herself to be like every other woman he'd been with—she wanted the whole white picket fence thing. And that was never going to be something he was going to be able to offer. All he could give was his love and she had turned him away.

For a fleeting second he wondered if it was all some act—was it possible she was only doing this out of fear?

He glanced around Bobby's Room, the area of the Bellagio set aside for high-stakes games. Vice was talking to the player to his right, almost as if purposefully trying to not interact with Three-Eyed Nate. As Chance turned, Nate sneered at him.

A crowd of onlookers had formed inside the doors that led into the room. A few cameras flashed, giving the room a strange party feel. Starling was once again huddled in a corner, concentrated on her book. Everyone was there for the multimillion-dollar show. Everyone except Harper.

If she did love him, she would have been down in the room, showing her support—she had to be done with Dr. McDougal by now. He tried to control some of his wavering emotions. Harper was helping Starling, he had to remember that. She was trying to help his daughter. Even if she didn't care about him, she did care about Starling. Very few times in his life had someone been so giving or so willing to help. The thought only made him want her more.

Looking to the door, he silently begged she would break through the crowd and meet him with a wanting smile, but he was only met with a burly man wearing black leather chaps leading a scared looking businessman around on a leash. Chance snorted as he remembered the businessman from the lobby when they had arrived.

Across the room from the Dom and his Sub, Kodie leaned against the wall as he talked with Mr. Blackwater and his bodyguard. Chance hated to think what they were talking about.

"Hey, Take-A-Chance, I hope you and Kodie have my money," Three-Eyed Nate growled from across the poker table as they waited for the game to begin.

The four other players stared at Chance like he was a sheep being led to slaughter. "We got it. Kodie is good to his word."

Chance tried not to stare up at the tattooed eye in the middle of Three-Eyed Nate's head. When Nate frowned the inked eye seemed to blink shut, the effect made Chance want to look away. It was a smart ploy by a poker player to use such a hideous diversion—the creepy eye was guaranteed to draw the focus away from the activity at the table, or in this case, the threat Nate posed.

The dealer shuffled the deck one more time and laid his hands down on the table, in true Vegas style. The player to the left of the dealer put out a blind, similar to an ante, and was followed with a big blind by the man to his left. The muffled sounds of slot machines and bells echoed into the room from the main casino floor.

Nerves crept up Chance's spine. This was it. Either they were going to win and pay back Nate, or they would have to trust the gaming commissioner to follow through on his end of the deal. A card slid across the felt and stopped at Chance's fingertips as the dealer made his way clockwise around the table.

Three-Eyed Nate leaned forward and lifted the edge of his cards. The fading tattoo on his forehead squinted, as if it too was trying to see the cards. The second card slid across the table and stopped at the edges of Chance's fingertips.

He flipped up the corners of the cards just far enough for him to see. He was met with a king of hearts and a king of spades. He had to check his smile, but he couldn't stop the thought of how even his cards were an omen. In a way they were just like him, he could be the king of love and romance, or he could be left with spades—the symbol of war. Love and war, together in his poker hand and in his life. Individually the cards were nothing, but together they were strong, powerful, and able to rule the table if he could play them well.

Or maybe he could have gotten their meaning all wrong. Maybe they meant he would have to fight for love in order to be the ruler of his own life.

He shook away the thoughts. They were nothing more than a couple of great cards, a pair of kings that would help him win the game ... or set up Nate's collusion as the gaming commissioner wanted. This night and the future of the people around him rested on his shoulders.

Vice and another of the players folded as the play passed around the table. Chance checked.

"Don't have the cards, eh, Take-a-Chance?" Three-Eyed Nate said, breaking the tense silence between the players.

Chance didn't take the bait. It was only the beginning, he had to play tight, but he had to play the hand he was dealt.

"I get it. You're used to playing with your little friend Kodie, aren't you?" The eye on Nate's forehead seemed to widen as the man gave a gape-mouthed laugh. Chance tried to ignore the man's jibes as the play continued around him. The game was going to be long if this was how Three-Eyed Nate was going to play.

The dealer burned a card, setting it to the side, and then dealt the flop cards. Queen of hearts, eight of hearts, and a two of diamonds.

Chance had three suited cards in hearts and the pair of kings. The odds were still in his favor.

Two more players folded, leaving only Chance and Three-Eyed Nate in the hand.

"Don't forget how much you owe me, Take-a-Chance," Nate chided.

It was going to be hard not to follow his gut and push Three-Eyed Nate's fat face into the felt. The only way Chance could win was to play tight, no emotions, no tells—and especially no anger. He couldn't let Three-Eyed Nate get under his skin.

He threw out a bet of ten thousand.

"Whew," Three-Eyed Nate said in an exhale. "Must have a damn fine hand." The man stared at Chance, waiting for him to make a mistake, but Nate would have to keep waiting—Chance was here to win.

Chance gave a shallow laugh. "Stay in or get out, it's up to you, but if you played like you did last year in the World Series of Poker Tournament, I'm sure you won't need to get too comfortable. You won't make it to the final two."

The dealer flipped the turn card. King of clubs. The king of the peasants. Perfect. Three of a kind with his pocket kings. Chance had the win almost regardless of what the last card, or the river, would bring.

Nate flipped up the corner of his cards.

"You gonna bet, or do I need to call time on you?"

"I have ninety seconds." Nate dropped down the corners of his cards. "Check."

Chance bet fifteen thousand. Nate drew his hands to his face, covering his mouth. After a few seconds, he reached down and threw in his cards, folding the hand.

"I hope you'll have enough cash left at the end of the game," Chance jabbed. "I'd hate for you to lose your ass."

Nate leaned back, even his tattooed eye seemed to glare at him. Chance took his time organizing the chips he'd won into four neat stacks. Mr. Blackwater took a step forward. Catching Chance's eye, he shook his head—reminding Chance of what all he had to lose.

•••

The door to the elevator opened and the couple standing in front of Harper and Dr. Redbird stepped out, leaving them alone.

Harper turned to face her enemy. "I just don't understand. You want to have a child, yes?"

Dr. Redbird answered with a tight nod.

"Well, if Jenna wasn't able to carry a child to term with GX 149, then what makes you think you'll be able to?"

The doctor's purse slipped on her shoulder and the woman jerked it back into place—allowing nothing out of control. "Don't think you are smarter than me … I just need the drugs and then I can figure out a way to have a child."

The elevator climbed, carrying them higher up the building.

"Clearly they didn't work for Jenna—and they probably won't work for you." Harper tried to keep her face straight as the thought of Jenna and her miscarriage came to the front of her mind. Suddenly it made sense, the drugs had helped with fertility, but in order for a pregnancy to be carried to term, the woman had to also mate with a god or demigod.

Harper's phone vibrated in her pocket. She pulled it out and studied the text. "Chance is playing," Starling had written.

"Give me that fucking thing." Dr. Redbird pulled the phone from Harper's hand and dropped it into her purse. "I don't need anyone getting any goddamn ideas. All I want is the drugs. What's so hard about this?"

Did Dr. Redbird understand the link? Did she know the missing requirement for carrying to term?

The elevator dinged and the car came to a stop at the thirty-fifth floor leading to the penthouse. She needed to get away from the doctor. She couldn't give the woman the drugs.

"I already know what you're missing," Harper said, attempting to entice Dr. Redbird away from her objective.

"What are you talking about?"

If Harper told the woman what she knew, she would be putting Chance in danger. Without a doubt the woman would go after him, taking what she needed to get what she desired. But Harper couldn't think of any way around this … She had a choice—give up Starling or give up Chance.

He had trusted her. He would never trust her again if she told his secret, but there was no other way. She couldn't let Starling's last lifeline, her drugs, be taken by this mad vulture-woman. Harper loved Chance, but she couldn't leave Starling with nothing. She'd made the girl a promise.

"If you let me keep the GX 149 in my possession, I have something else, something better, I can offer in its place."

"What do you mean?" Dr. Redbird eyed her suspiciously. "The medication worked. Starling is proof of that. Why would I want anything else?"

"But the drugs didn't work for Jenna. And there's a reason. Even if I give you the drugs, they aren't going to work, but if you let me keep them I will help you."

The elevator door opened. Sticking out her foot, Dr. Redbird held open the door and stared at the penthouse's door.

"I want the GX 149. Dr. McDougal told me there was no more—you had the only supply left. I can't go back without them. They won't stop looking until I get them."

Harper shuddered as she wondered who *they* were. Dr. Redbird made it sound like she was the one who wanted the drugs, but were there others? Were others behind her search? Was that why she had become so desperate?

The world seemed to clear around her. Dr. Redbird wasn't acting alone.

"I know you need the drugs. But if you give me time, maybe I can replicate the chemical compounds—that way we all have what we need. That's what Dr. McDougal and I were working on before … before you killed him."

The woman stuffed her hands around her body like a petulant child. "He knew the cost of his defiance. And you should know too. If you are lying to me, or if you try to deceive me, I will not only kill you, but I'll kill your friends as well."

Not if Harper could kill the doctor first. "I get it, but I'm not trying to defy you, I'm only trying to help you," she lied. "Are you going to leave the drugs with me and let me do my research? Or are you willing to risk it all?"

"If I take the drugs, I risk nothing and I get what I want."

"For now. But what happens if you don't get pregnant right away? You killed the only other person besides me who can help you get more. You'll just end up where you started—frustrated, and unable to have a baby."

As the words sank in, the woman's face tightened. "Shut up," Dr. Redbird scowled. "Just give me the drugs. There's no way you can help me. If you knew the secret, you would have helped your sister instead of letting her get killed. Don't think you will get away with playing me for some kind of fool."

Grabbing Harper, the woman shoved her out of the elevator. "Go get me the drugs. Now. No more screwing around."

No one got away with touching her like that—least of all the little vulture-shifter. "Fine."

Harper reached into her purse and drew out the penthouse key and slid it into the lock. The woman couldn't get the drugs. She couldn't threaten the people Harper cared about. She couldn't win.

The door opened with a click.

Harper walked through the doorway toward the overstuffed gold chairs. The door slammed shut behind her. The noise echoed through the room and Harper turned with a start. Standing behind the door, to the doctor's right, was a man. He rushed at Dr. Redbird, setting her off balance as he drove his shoulder into her chest. She flew backward into the small table by the door with a surprised, garbled scream. The vase of fresh cut flowers flew from the table and crashed, spreading glass and water like sparkling tears across the hardwood floor.

Amongst the spray of tears was Dr. Redbird's purse. Dr. McDougal's manila envelope, the key to Starling's future, stuck out of the top. Harper stepped over and grabbed the envelope and stuck it under her arm.

She moved to stand as she noticed, in the middle of a pile of broken glass, the small white syringe. Almost in a trance, Harper stepped over to the needle, barely noticing the wrestling bodies behind her.

Through the thin plastic of the syringe, a small bubble wiggled its way to the top, struggling as it tried to break from its trap. Picking up the syringe, she pulled the orange cap from its tip and stared at the sharp point of the instrument. It was so small. This thing in her hands seemed almost innocuous, so unlikely to hurt, but she knew the truth. Dr. Redbird had killed and she wouldn't stop killing until she got what she wanted. There was no end to the pain she would inflict if she got her way. There was only one way to stop a mad woman like her.

Harper turned back. The man was on top of Dr. Redbird, his dark hair fell into his sweat-covered face. Dr. Redbird reached up and drew her nails down his face. "You bitch," he yelled, pushing down her hand, he wrapped his leg around hers and flipped her over in one clean motion. Jerking her hands behind her back, he reached down to his waist and pulled out a zip tie. Blood rose from the gashes on his cheek and started to descend down the tan skin of his young, early-twenties face.

"Jasper?" Harper moved toward the pair.

"What are you doing?" the young man asked, wrapping the zip tie around Dr. Redbird's wrists and pulling it tight.

"She has to die."

He looked at the woman who lay between his legs. "The sisterhood wants her to live. They don't want a war."

"No one is going to fight for this woman. She's evil." Harper took another step and raised the needle like it was a knife and she only needed to let it plunge.

Dr. Redbird twisted under his legs and looked back toward Harper. "You slut. You and your kind are going to pay for this. If you kill me, I vow that every last Catharterian will come after you and your little Starling." She jerked and looked back at the man. "You assholes are nothing."

"Give me the needle." The man stuck out his hand.

Harper let the needle lower. "She needs to die. She can't be trusted. If we don't kill her now she will never quit coming after us."

"You need to trust me." He pointed at the needle. "Give it to me."

The glass crunched under Harper's feet as she took the last step. Jasper pulled the needle from her fingers.

He lowered the needle. Its silver tip plunged into the dilated vein protruding from the woman's reddened neck.

"No!" Dr. Redbird thrashed between the man's legs, but his muscle-riddled body tensed and held the woman in place. He pushed the plunger down. The bubble in the liquid moved downward and disappeared, passing from one death trap to another.

Chapter Twenty-Four

The cards were falling Chance's way, but it seemed like however he played he couldn't get ahead—something was wrong. The men had to be cheating, as Mr. Blackwater had assumed. There was no way, with Chance's luck, that he could be losing so badly. Reaching forward, Chance picked up two ten thousand dollar chips and posted the small blind. Vice followed, posting the twenty thousand dollar big blind.

The dealer picked up the cards and dealt out the remaining three players' two pocket cards. Vice's aviator sunglasses reflected the lights as he leaned forward and lifted the corner of his cards. He glanced in Chance's direction and his body tensed.

As the man pulled his hands back from his pocket cards, his fingers tapped on the felt table. If he hadn't been watching, Chance would have certainly missed the signal. He glanced over toward Nate. He was leaning back in his chair a smug grin on his face, but they hadn't gotten away with anything. "I'll play. Call," Nate said, setting a twenty thousand dollar stack out to match the big blind.

By most standards the bet would have been questionable, but the bet was enough to make Chance wonder what Nate held in his pocket cards. If it had been nothing, the bet would have been smaller. Whatever Nate held, and his partner had signaled, was enough to make him feel confident to play the round.

The doors to the room opened a little wider and Harper squeezed through the mass of bystanders who crowded the doorway. Behind her walked a dark-haired man with deep scratches down his cheek, which he tried to cover with even darker sunglasses, almost matching the ones often worn by poker players. The man was up to something. Chance could see it in his stride, almost like he was the boss, except he looked as if he waited for the hammer to fall.

Harper had only been supposed to meet Dr. McDougal and get the drugs. This man didn't seem like the doctor type. Instead he seemed more like the type that Chance needed to worry about—the type who would steal the woman he loved. If he hadn't been required to sit there and play the hand, if he hadn't been trying to help out the gaming commissioner by taking down the two men who shared the table, he would have been at her side in an instant.

Kodie caught his gaze and Chance motioned toward Harper and the unwelcome stranger at her side. Kodie made a beeline to the pair.

"She's a fine piece of ass, Take-a-Chance," Three-Eyed Nate said with a grating laugh as he motioned toward Harper. "I don't know what she would be doing here, looking at you like that."

"She's not here for me."

Chance caught Harper's gaze. Her mouth formed into words, but he couldn't understand what she tried to say.

"What're you gonna do, Take-a-Chance? Monitor traffic all day long? Or are you gonna bet?" Nate signaled the dealer. "Let's play the clock here. I know it's hard to make up your mind when you aren't the best."

He lifted the corner of his cards exposing the ace of hearts and king of hearts, which rested in his pocket hand. The cards couldn't be any better, but it all would depend on the flop. Even if the other men were cheating, he still had a chance to win and make the damn cheaters wish they'd never tried to tip him over.

"Call," Chance said, as he laid another ten thousand dollars into the pot, matching the bet of the players around him. He tried to play it cool and not tip them off to the potentially lethal blow his hand could deliver. He needed to wait for the moment to strike.

"Call." Vice scratched the tip of his nose. Everything the man did, every action he took, seemed unnatural, almost forced. The men in security and the pit bosses had to be seeing what was going on.

Chance had seen cheaters before, but these cheaters were highly skilled. Watching them in action it was tough to tell exactly what was happening, and had he not been tipped off, he would have probably been just like Kodie, falling victim to their entrapment.

The dealer burned a card, then started to deal the flop cards.

Ten of hearts. Perfect, only two more well-placed hearts and he would have the best hand in poker.

Ace of diamonds. Diamonds were said to be a girl's best friend, but in this case they were his. At the very least, if all the other cards fell through, he now sat on a high pair of aces.

The dealer flipped the last card. Jack of spades. A little of his hope drifted away into the black pool of ink that littered the card.

He would need two more hearts to have a flush and maybe the power position. He had a strong hand, but for a moment he considered folding. The two cheaters could have the table to themselves, bidding away against each other. He could use the time to his advantage, waiting until the moment one pushed the other out of the game. But it would cost him. He'd have to keep posting the blinds. It would get expensive.

He placed a chip on his pocket cards. "Check." If he didn't bet big, he could watch the men and gauge the cards in their hands. They wanted his money, they wanted to beat him, but were they willing to put themselves at risk in doing it?

Vice's lips twitched, almost in disgust. "Check."

Three-Eyed Nate's buggy little third eye scrunched as he scowled. "Bunch of chicken shits, I see." He motioned to the dealer. "Check."

The pair must have been waiting to see what the turn would bring, waiting to see if they could keep him in the game.

The dealer burned a card and turned over the turn card. Queen of hearts. The true gauge of a great poker player was their ability to forecast what was in the other players' hands. And right now, the best either of the other players could hope for was a straight, or they could be going for the heart flush as well. Who held the winning hand would all come down to the river.

Vice and Nate had the advantage of watching Chance's bet to gauge the power of his hand—and they could bet accordingly. But this was also his opportunity to take control of the table and draw on the pair's greed, by making them think he had a questionable hand.

Chance needed to set himself up for the bluff in the next round of betting. "Check." If they wanted his money, they were going to have to come after it.

He could sense Vice's icy gaze on him, checking him for weakness. "I'll bet forty thousand." His chips clicked as he placed them into neat stacks in the center of the table.

"Is that how you're gonna play, Chance?" Nate chided. "A little weak for you, ain't it?"

He smiled. "Gotta take a ride on the river, you know how it is."

"No, I don't know *how it is*. I'll raise your bet, Vice … Another sixty thousand." Nate took a stack of chips and counted out a hundred thousand dollars.

Chance's gut clenched.

"I'll call your bet and raise you another twenty thousand." He refused to let his fingers tremble in excitement and nervousness as he counted one hundred and twenty thousand dollars in chips. The little stack looked unimpressive, but added to the pot, it made it clear how much this hand could come to matter.

Vice picked up a few chips. "I'll call."

"You won't win that easy. I'm in," Nate said.

The dealer burned the top card. Chance stared at the dealer's hands, silently begging for the jack of hearts. If the jack turned on the river he would have the best hand in poker—a royal flush. If not, he would be left only to hope for a heart for the flush. If the card was black, the best he could hope for was that he hadn't wasted more of his money betting on a pair of aces.

The card flipped with a flash of black. Chance sucked in a breath. No …

Ace of spades. His hopes came crashing down. Three aces. It wasn't a bad hand, but it was far from the best. They were both still betting, but since they were cheating it was likely that Vice or Nate, the one with the lower hand, was only pushing up the bet, hoping to get as much money as possible.

Maybe he should have folded, but it was too late now.

He needed a strong bet, one that spoke to the probability his cards were good, but small enough that he could still keep playing. If he lost this hand, he would only have two hundred thousand left. If Vice and Nate continued to work together that money would be gone in a flash. He had to play like this was it— everything came down to this last round of bets. "One hundred thousand."

Vice pushed his sunglasses up the bridge of his nose. "I'll raise you by sixty thousand."

Just as he had assumed, Vice was pushing up the bet. If Vice folded in the next round of betting it would prove they were trying to control the table and steal his money. Chance looked up at the ceiling where a black bubble filled with cameras silently stared down. They better be watching.

Three-Eyed Nate lifted the corner of his cards, the action pensive, but it was all a ploy to pull Chance deeper into the game. "I can beat that, Vice. I raise." He slid in two hundred thousand dollars like he was pushing away a plate after a large meal.

To continue playing, Chance would have to put up another hundred thousand dollars, only leaving him with a hundred thousand for the next hand, should he lose. Or he could go all in and hope and pray that he had the best hand. They were forcing him to move—out of the game or all in.

"I'm all in." He counted out his remaining chips. "Two hundred thousand," he said, sliding them into the mountain of chips at the center.

Vice let out a whistle through the center of his teeth. "Whew, you must have one hell of a hand." He lifted the corner of his cards. "I'm out." He lifted the cards and threw them into the muck.

Nate gave him a wild smile. Chance hated the feeling of being right where the cheaters wanted—at their mercy. "I'll call," Nate slid in the necessary chips and leaned back in his chair.

A lump formed in Chance's throat. The security guards weren't coming. Vice and Nate had gotten away with the collusion. Had he been the one being set up? Had the gaming commissioner played him for a fool and made him think the two men were plotting against him, when in reality they hadn't? Had he gotten it all wrong?

Had he just lost everything?

He flipped over his pocket cards. Three of a kind.

Nate's wild smile grew even larger, taking on the look of some strange god, the way his tattooed eye seemed to stretch and contort over his forehead.

"What is it, Nate? You got it beat?" Chance asked, tapping nervously on his cards.

Nate picked up his cards.

"Watch out! Excuse me!" A group of men and women rushed through the doors. The letters NPD were emblazoned on the chests of their brown police uniforms. "Vice Dalton and Nate Berkshire, you are under arrest for gambling fraud, cheating at gambling, and attempting to cheat and conspiracy to cheat."

The cards slipped from Nate's fingers. Queen of clubs. King of spades. Nate had gotten a straight.

Chance had lost it all.

Chapter Twenty-Five

The gaming commissioner's office was filled with bland tan-colored filing cabinets. Above them on the walls was picture after picture of Mr. Blackwater standing, unsmiling, with the big names of poker and several professional football players.

"Thank you for your cooperation, Chance." Mr. Blackwater stepped behind his leather office chair and leaning down, opened his desk's drawer.

"I thought you were going to leave me hanging," Chance admitted. "I was damn glad when I saw the police walking through the doors."

"I'm sure you were," Mr. Blackwater said, motioning for his bodyguard to close the office door. "But I'm always good to my word. I'm just glad I didn't have to follow through on my threat."

"So am I," Chance said, shifting uncomfortably from one foot to the other. He hadn't ever intended on going against the commissioner, but he couldn't help but imagine standing out in the desert just waiting for the bodyguard to place the bullet.

"As you know by now, Nate and Vice will be spending a significant amount of time in jail. I know you wish to keep your name out of the press for taking an active role in taking them down, but a debt is owed." Blackwater slid the drawer shut. "When the police searched Nate's home, they found proof that not only were they cheating the casinos out of millions of dollars, but they were also teaching other poker players how to run scams. You saved us from losing millions more. As a thank you, the Vegas casinos, including the Bellagio, have pooled some money."

Mr. Blackwater lifted up the familiar silver briefcase. "Inside, not only will you find the five hundred thousand dollars from your tournament buy-in, but you will also find an additional six million. We hope you will return to our casinos with the knowledge you are always welcome."

"You just want me to come back and spend the money at your casinos," Chance said with a relieved chuckle.

"Hey, casinos are the imperfect heart of this city. I'm sure you know how far we are from being saints." Mr. Blackwater picked up a pen from his desk and clicked the end, exposing the nib. "Speaking of saints, I just found out some interesting news about what was going on while the tournament was taking place. Have you had a chance to talk to any of your acquaintances yet?"

It had been a flurry of action. First the police, then the onslaught of questions from curious bystanders, he'd only barely escaped Bobby's Room when Mr. Blackwater's bodyguard had ushered him from the tournament. "No, I haven't seen my friends since the police arrived."

Mr. Blackwater almost smiled. "Well, Chance, we found not one, but two dead bodies in our hotel. In fact, your friend Harper was seen coming out of the rooms where the murdered individuals were found."

What had Harper done?

"I'm sure she had nothing to do with either of the deaths," Chance said, forcing an edge of cold, calm indifference into his voice.

"I think if you dug a little deeper, you would find that we are not far off the mark."

If the gaming commissioner called the police it would spell disaster for Harper. How could she possibly explain being seen coming out of two different murder scenes? She could never tell the authorities about the drugs, or who she really was—they would punish her to the fullest extent of the law. "What are you going to do?"

"Well, Chance, your little friend cost us no money, aside for the fee to keep a few people silent about depositing the bodies in the sand. Let's call this little incident with your girlfriend a professional courtesy. It won't happen again, but this time we are willing to let a few things slide."

Everything came with a price.

"And?"

"And what? You saved us millions. We can ignore a few inconvenient truths … Perhaps."

"I've known you long enough, Mr. Blackwater, to realize that this isn't the end of it. What's your angle?"

One corner of Mr. Blackwater's mouth finally turned up into what Chance was sure was the man's finest smile. "You do know me well."

"So?"

"Well, we are looking for a new professional poker player who is willing to call our casino home for a while. We are hoping to pull new international games to our tables. We've come to the decision you might just be the man we are looking for."

Once again, the man held him in a position that only left one choice. "So you want me to be your pet poker player?"

"It's up to you. But I bet that … " He pointed at a note on his desk with two names scrawled beneath. "Dr. Eliot McDougal's family would be interested to learn your acquaintance is responsible for his death."

If Chance took the job he would be at Mr. Blackwater's beck and call. If he didn't, Harper would be carted to prison. He loved her too much to let something like that happen. Even if she didn't love him.

"I'm in. I'll take the job. On one condition … ."

"And what is that?"

"First, I get to finish raising my daughter."

Chapter Twenty-Six

The entire trip they had talked about what had transpired in the hotel. Harper talked about Dr. McDougal's tragic death and his cryptic warning about Jenna's keys and how she still needed to find the books her sister had left behind. Chance talked about the game, and the turn of the cards. Kodie talked about the excitement of watching Nate and Vice being taken away in handcuffs. Starling talked about ghosts and all the things she had seen in Vegas, her favorite of which had been going to the Bellagio fountains with Jasper Gray—she kept calling them *enchanting*.

The one thing that none of them talked about was the future. Each of them seemed to sidestep the subject with uncomfortable silence or jarring conversational turns. No one wanted to talk about what was going to come.

Jenna's little white 1950s house sat on the quiet Idaho street, lonesome and lifeless. Harper couldn't help the thought that she was so much like this house. Her future looked dull as she thought of life without Chance, Starling, and Kodie. At least she had finally succeeded in helping the people she loved.

She glanced over at Chance. The fine lines around his eyes seemed to have deepened on their trip.

The truck came to a stop in the driveway. "I guess we're here," Chance said, finally breaking the heavy silence that seemed to have only grown as they had neared Worley.

"You are coming in, aren't you?" Harper asked, but her heart was tearing apart. This was the last time she was going to see them. They had no reason to stay together. She had nothing to offer any of them, nothing except her love.

"That would be great," Kodie spoke up from the back seat. "Let's go, Starling. Let's give these guys a minute."

Harper turned and gave Kodie an appreciative smile even though her stomach was spinning. "Here," she said, reaching into her purse and pulling out the key to the house. "You'll need this."

Kodie grabbed the key and opened the door to the truck. Starling scooted near and leaned into Harper's ear. "A wise woman once told me it's important to know when you need to fight," she whispered. "Fight for love."

Starling stepped out of the truck with Kodie's help. The way her pale fingers fit into Kodie's aged hand reminded Harper of how much she was going to miss them. Kodie and his love of life. Starling and her maturity and ill-fitting adolescence. And Chance. She would miss Chance most of all …

The truck's door clicked shut behind Kodie and Starling. Starling gave her one last smile before they disappeared into the house.

Starling was right. She had to fight. It was now or never.

Chance reached over and took her hand. He stared out the windshield, unable to meet her gaze.

She wanted to fight, yes, but she had no idea what she was going to say—or if he wanted the same things she did, especially after she had told him that she didn't love him.

It seemed impossible to make things better. But if she didn't do something, she was going to miss him. She was going to miss the way his hands always seemed to find hers when she needed his touch the most. She was going to miss the way his eyes lit up when she entered the room. More than that, she was going to miss the feeling that filled her every time he was near. These feelings … This love … was going to be unforgettable.

Opening up her purse, she reached inside and pulled out Dr. McDougal's envelope. "Here, Chance."

"What's this?" he asked, taking the envelope and opening it up. He pulled out the papers and stared at them as if they were written in Greek. "What does this mean?"

"It's the chemical formula for GX 149."

"What?" His smile caught fire and spread to his eyes. "How did you get this?"

"Dr. Redbird … dropped it."

"Harper, you promise you didn't kill her?"

"No." She smiled. "Jasper did."

"Starling's friend?" Chance asked, his voice filled with a strange mixture of relief and annoyance.

Harper nodded. "He was sent by the sisterhood, and he's going to be following Starling until we can make sure everything is safe from the Catharterians—the vulture-shifter group."

"What am I supposed to do with the formula?" Chance lifted the papers. "You're the only person who can help us."

"I was thinking with your winnings you can pay a laboratory to make more of the drug. Make sure only someone you truly trust has access to the formula."

The papers scratched as he slid them back inside the envelope. "Thank you, for everything … "

"I made Starling a promise. I couldn't let her down."

"Have you forgiven yourself, Harper?"

"For what?" There were a million things he could have been talking about.

"For Jenna's death?"

His question came out of left field, hitting her like a glancing blow. Yet, for the first time, it didn't hurt. It didn't feel like her heart was going to break into a million pieces with the thoughts of her sister.

"I don't know, but having you and Starling in my life has made it all more bearable." She paused. "I guess I haven't forgiven myself, and I may never forgive myself. But Jenna made her own choices, and it's time for me to move forward."

A tired sadness overtook the fire in his eyes. "Are you going to go back to Seattle?"

For a moment she was back standing in the sterile, austere walls of the lab, spending twelve hours a day sequestered away in the lonely world of science. The thought made her shudder.

"No, Chance. I can't go back." She grabbed hold of the door handle like she was holding on in an effort not to lose control of her feelings. "I can't go back to being alone … or being without you."

Chance gave her a sexy, unbridled smile. "Are you sure? Are you really willing to give up your work?"

Harper answered with a slow nod. "I want you to make me one promise. Starling needs to stay in Worley. She only has six months left of school. She can stay here with me until she gets done. She needs to get help before she has to face the world alone. She needs to be surrounded by love. Okay?"

"That's fine, but I want … *us* too," Chance said. "I'll stay here with you and Starling … hell, I'll even let Kodie stay if he wants. We can have our own family. And I can give up poker—I'll figure out something to make Blackwater happy—I'll give him his money back … whatever it takes. But if you want, I'll stop so we can all be together."

"Chance, you and I both know you wouldn't be happy if you stopped playing poker. It's what makes you happy—it's your passion. I don't ever want you to regret your decision in giving it up to be with me. Regret turns into resentment and I won't let you do that to yourself. I love you too much to ask you to change. When it's time to go to Vegas, I'll go with you. Maybe I can find another job if I want … I have a feeling Shaw is going to be hiring."

"Did you say you love me?" He smiled his irresistible million-dollar smile.

Butterflies rose in her belly. "I do. I love you—"

"I love you, too. You stole my heart the second you tripped over the barstool." The heaviness that had seemed to weigh upon his shoulders lifted and he leaned toward her. His lips met hers.

She couldn't say no. Not to his kiss, not to his love, and least of all to a new life. The life she had been waiting to start.

"Be with me ... for the rest of time," Chance said in between kisses.

"Yes, Chance ... Yes ... "

A ray of sunshine burst into the pickup, warming the space with its welcomed brightness. For so long she had been a lonely swan, trapped in the darkness of the winter in her heart. Her only solace had been her work and the security that came with the rhythmic passage of time. No longer. No longer could she be a winter swan. The love for Chance and his young daughter had brought an unexpected spring to her life. More than spring, she had found the things she needed above all else—she'd found love and a family.

Epilogue

The door to Harper sister's house slammed shut behind Starling, catching her off-guard and she stumbled into the small table. A set of keys tumbled to the ground. The house was in disarray, boxes were strewn across the floor, their contents spilling out like poorly kept secrets.

Starling bent down and picked up the ring of mismatched keys—next to them was a little, broken porcelain doll, its painted on smile still intact. A brass key slipped to the front of the ring, catching Starling's attention. On the key's little brass surface was engraved the words: "Do not duplicate. First National Bank, Savannah, GA."

Her mother had once owned a key that had looked like this little brass one. Carey had once said it belonged to a safe deposit box.

Standing up, she was just about to drop the keys back onto the table next to a crystal swan when she spotted a jumbled stack of letters. On the top of the pile sat an unopened envelope. At the top left corner, in the sender location, it read *First National Bank … Savannah, Georgia …*

Open it … . A ghostly voice echoed through her, drawing chills to her skin. She hated when *they* spoke to her. Writing was so much easier. When she had been on full doses of GX 149 the voices had been quiet, but now she was rationing the supply and the voices had returned, stronger than ever.

Open it … .

No … She thought. *Quit talking to me. You're not welcome.*

Open it … .

They wouldn't stop. Not spirits. Not when they had come to her.

Carefully, as to not draw Kodie's attention as he made his way to the empty prehistoric kitchen, she tore the edge of the envelope and opened the letter.

She started to read.

Dear Ms. Cygnini;

We have included a copy of your Petition to Open Safe Deposit Box. In addition to your power of attorney's signature, they will need to provide:

Will to probate court where bank is located

Deed to burial plot or burial instructions to petitioner

We appreciate your business and look forward to working with you in the future.

It didn't make any sense. Why would a spirit want her to read the letter? It was just another bank letter.

Find the books in the box … Find the books and find answers …

Why? She thought, sending her question to the spirit.

There was no answer.

She had no right to take Jenna's or Harper's property, but as she questioned her actions a cold spread through her, the sign of a ghost manifestation. The spirit pressed its icy fingers around her warm hand and gave it a slight push, urging her to take the letter.

Kodie whistled away in the kitchen, blissfully unaware of her inner turmoil. She had to trust the spirit. There was a reason it wanted her to act. Starling slipped the keys into her purse. Harper had tried to help her and she had promised to continue trying to isolate the chemicals in the GX 149, but Starling had never been the kind to hold out hope to be saved by another. She was her own woman. She couldn't *wait* to be rescued.

About the Author

Danica Winters is a bestselling author who is known for writing award-winning books that grip readers with their ability to drive emotion through suspense and often a touch of magic. When she's not working, she can be found in the wilds of Montana testing her patience while she tries to understand the allure of various crafts (quilting, pottery, and painting are not her thing). She always believes the cup is neither half full nor half empty, but it better be filled with wine.

Please feel free to contact her through her website: *www. DanicaWinters.net*
Facebook: *www.Facebook.com/DanicaWinters*
Twitter: *www.Twitter.com/DanicaWinters*

More from This Author
(From *Montana Mustangs* by Danica Winters)

The waves of the lake crashed next to Dane Burke like greedy reporters descending onto a crime scene. Dane picked up the severed hand, careful to touch it only with the tips of his gloved fingers, all in an attempt to save what little evidence remained.

The fingers were wrinkled and pale, the color of rotting fish. The skin of the palm flapped back, exposing the white lines of the tendons and the bloated pink muscles of the victim's hand. He pushed back the skin, covering the hand's viscera. The flesh was rubbed raw in several places, but whether it was from the time in the water or something else Dane couldn't be sure.

Behind him, the secondary officer, Grant, talked with the woman who'd phoned in the find. The woman was blonde, thin, and uncomfortably beautiful.

"So, Aura, are you in Montana for business or pleasure?" Officer Grant asked, with just a little too much glee in his voice.

Dane tried to ignore the amateurish come-ons the officer threw at the blonde with the large blue eyes and plump lips that pulsed with the pink hues of life.

He turned the gruesome hand over in his. The fingernails of the victim were painted a vivid red, now brighter than the blood that had settled in the person's flesh. He snickered quietly as he thought about the stark difference between the woman behind him who was the embodiment of life and the macabre sloughing object of death he stared upon.

Maybe the kid wasn't so wrong for focusing on the woman. If he'd been just a few years younger, maybe he would have been acting that way too—focusing on the beauty of the woman instead of the gore of the job. But he'd long since given up on the things in life that only brought bitterness—death was easier to handle.

Officer Grant mumbled something, and his laughter bounced off the black lake and disappeared into the still of the night. Yet, the woman stayed silent—making Dane like her just a little bit more for avoiding the stupidity that Grant kept unchecked.

This crime scene was going to be one hell of a mess—between the identification and then locking down suspects; the case was going to have to be the focus of his life. He hadn't had a possible homicide for two years. The last case had been cut and dry; man beat his wife, wife murdered husband—mitigated murder. She got two years in prison, a slap on the wrist.

Today all he had was a mutilated hand. Unidentifiable until the DNA came in, no one missing—at least, no one who had been reported missing—and no easy answers. Only one thing seemed likely—there would be a body to follow, but when and if it showed up was a mystery.

Whatever had happened to this woman could only be found in her flesh, unless someone popped up who had witnessed the event. If he had to guess, the hand had been in the water at least a few days. If someone had seen the possible murder, they would turn up soon or not at all.

The skin slipped in his, forcing him to grip it tighter. He laid the evidence down on the bag.

Dealing with suicides and natural deaths was something he did on a regular basis. Yet something about the rotting fish-hand made him shudder. Maybe it was the vibrant party-goer red nail polish and the way it made him think of some of the questionable women he had dated; or it could have been the way it had been removed from the body.

He stood up and wiped off the pebbles from his knees.

"Officer Grant, did you find anything else besides the hand?"

"Excuse me, Ms. Montgarten," the young brown-haired officer said with an overly warm smile.

The woman, Aura, was pretty and all, but the way the kid fawned made him want to gag. The woman was just another person in the long line of crazies they saw each and every day. Polite was fine, but *come on*.

The woman stared down at the hand at Dane's feet.

Officer Grant reached over and touched the woman's arm. "Don't worry about the hand now."

The woman jerked back and away from the boy's touch.

Dane held back the urge to snigger.

She pulled her arms around her body as an icy fall Montana wind blew up off the lake. "Why don't you take her to your car, Officer Grant?" Dane said. "She looks cold."

"No." She glared back at him. "I'm fine."

For a person who'd found the hand floating along the shoreline she seemed oddly quiet. She'd barely spoken since Dane had arrived on scene. Highly suspicious, and if he had to guess, she was the primary suspect. Most people loved to help, to talk away while they explained the crime procedures they had witnessed on *CSI* or some other bullshit television show, but not this woman.

Officer Grant nodded. "I'll grab you a blanket. Deputy Burke is right, you look cold. Can't have you freezing on us."

"I'll just wait in my truck." She spun on her boot's heel and stomped off to her late-model black Dodge towing a white horse trailer.

Officer Grant watched her as she fled from them.

"Grant, you gonna help in the investigation or drool over the blonde all day?"

"Sorry, Deputy. Just wanted to make sure our witness was comfortable."

Comfortable or doable? The kid didn't stand a chance with the woman.

"Did she give you any useable information?"

"Just said she had stopped at the marina and came across the hand."

"Did she say if she saw anyone else around?"

Officer Grant shook his head. "Sounds like there's been no one here but her."

Dane exhaled and watched as his breath made a whirling cloud in the cold air. Of course no one would be around on an evening like this. The lake was too cold, too deep for anyone to be out. "Did she say what she was doing here?"

"Just stopped for a rest."

Stopped for a rest at a marina? There was a campground only ten miles farther down the highway and not much further than that was a line of motels. Signs dotted the roadway advertising the various options to rest. Something didn't add up. "Where's she from?"

"Didn't say."

Rookie …

"Stay here with the evidence. Keep an eye on it. I'm going to go run through some questions with her."

"Sure, Deputy."

From the tone of the kid's voice it was easy to tell he was steadily making another friend in the office. Grant was free to add his name to the ever growing list of people that didn't like Dane Burke. The list was long and distinguished, with several county officials at the top. Dane had never been one to kiss ass or pander to the fickle moods of the politics that ran rampant through this tiny county in the northwest corner of Montana.

The beam of the flashlight bounced over the ground as Dane made his way to the black pickup parked under the lone street lamp. The plates were from Arizona. She was a long way from home.

The woman stared down at a map that lay in her lap as he stepped up to the window. He tapped on the glass with the end of his metal flashlight.

She looked up and shoved the map closed as she rolled down the window. "Officer?" Her cheeks flushed.

"It's Deputy Burke." He pointed to his name badge.

Her overly large eyes sparkled, making him shift uncomfortably in his work boots. "Deputy."

An odd trickle of guilt invaded him. She was suspicious, but he didn't need to be rude—he had worked for his reputation as an even-tempered cop and he didn't need to blow it on one good looking blonde. "Or you can call me Dane. That's my name, Dane Burke."

Great. He mentally groaned. *Now I sound like a freaking idiot.*

"*Dane.*" The corner of her mouth turned up in a little grin. "How can I help you? I think I already answered most of the other deputy's questions."

He pulled a notepad out of his front pocket. "I just have a few more questions for you. Make sure we get all of our bases covered."

She responded with a tight nod.

"Where exactly did you say you were from?"

"I'm just traveling through."

"From Arizona?"

Her blue eyes sparked. "Yeah. Right. Arizona."

So this was how she was going to play it? Like she was some kind of hard ass?

A little dream catcher dangled from her rearview mirror. The blue feather attached to the circle fluttered lazily in the breeze that filtered through the open window.

He clicked his pen and wrote down the word Arizona and her license plate number in a tight scrawl. "Where are you headed to?"

"What does it matter to your case? I told the other officer everything I know. I stopped, found the hand, and I called you guys. That's it. Nothing more."

What was she hiding? He instinctively put on his game face. No emotion, no tells.

"Do you have a horse in the back?" He pointed at the double horse trailer she was towing behind the three-quarter ton.

She glanced down at the side view mirror. "No."

"You moving?" He leaned back and aimed the flashlight at the trailer, but the light was swallowed by the darkness.

"The trailer's empty." Her eyes scanned the mirror again, sparking his inner-cop.

"You mind if I take a look?"

"Do you have a search warrant?"

The woman knew her rights. There was nothing he could do. She may not have had anything to do with the pale, bloated hand that rested on the shore, but there was no question about it, she was hiding something. And even if it killed him, he was going to find out.

Also from this author, check out The Nymph's Labryinth
In the mood for more Crimson Romance?
Check out *Witch's Revenge*
by Denyse Cohen
at *CrimsonRomance.com.*